A Long Memory

Sonia Dees

Contents

Chapter 1

Nina stared out the open window as she sat at her desk, the light breeze sweeping through her cropped, dark curls, like soft breaths against her sienna toned skin. The scents of the city—the petrichor smell after the morning's light rain—all converged in her mind, painting a bright picture. It was—she hoped—one that would not fade from her mind all too soon.

"The commissioner of the FDA is still in critical condition after the attempt on his life . . . " Nina only paid minimal attention to the anchor's voice filtering through the speakers of the screen mounted on the living room wall. The woman's tone was clear and detached from whatever breaking news she was rattling off despite the faint and painfully forced expression of concern she put on for the viewers. Nina had little interest for it all.

Her mind was still replaying a strange dream she'd had the previous night, though it was not the first. She recalled with startling clarity the hallways she'd walked down in her dream; walls painted a cream color, soft lighting reflecting off the polished hardwood floor. Nina had walked down the hall with a tune she couldn't quite recall playing from somewhere nearby and the scent of some type of flower she had yet to recognize hanging in the air. Then, there was the painting, some landscape painted in bold, warm tones yet still giving off a soothing sort of mood.

Nina had the strange feeling of familiarity when she thought back to the dream, despite her never having been to such a place. For a while, she thought of what the dream—so simple and yet refusing to leave her mind—might have meant, and could come up with no explanation. In the end, Nina had pushed any thoughts of it to the back of her mind, crediting the dream to her subconscious dealing with all that had happened to her as of late.

At the moment, she just marveled at the fact that she could recall with perfect clarity what she'd had for breakfast the previous day. The crunch of the toast and the nearly overwhelming sweetness of the marmalade, mixing with the scent of freshly brewed coffee, still so vivid she could almost taste it all. Nina could even recall the way the morning sunlight had filtered through the blinds as they slowly opened at the usual time and the insurance commercial that played when the television turned on as she walked into the living room.

It was, as strange as it would seem to the average person, an amazing feeling to remember. Nina didn't think it was something she'd ever take for granted.

". . . Fearnley is currently awaiting trial for the slaying of Alice Cassill. . . ."

"Incoming call from Iris." The notification jolted Nina from her thoughts even as she answered without thinking using a simple voice command.

Iris was a friend of hers and co-worker. Her cheery greeting made Nina smile and she realized at that moment that she had missed the daily interactions with all the people she worked with. Iris, in particular, had always been good company.

"How are you feeling?" Iris asked, voice streaming through the small speaker in Nina's living room. It rang clearly through the room even as Nina moved away from the window and to the small kitchenette.

"Great. I've been doing nothing but resting so that's not surprising." Nina didn't mention the headaches, nor the strange dreams she'd had, didn't think they mattered enough. After all, most medical procedures and medications came with side effects. She didn't think it'd be so surprising to have her neuroprosthesis be the same. "How's work been?"

"Not the same without you around," Iris said, and Nina could hear the smile she must have worn as she spoke. "I swear, you always have the best articles. Gemma's been complaining about it now that you're not around. When are you coming back?"

"In about a week, maybe less if I get bored enough." Nina poured herself a glass of water and moved to the couch in the living room. There was an amused smile on her face at the thought of her boss hassling everyone due to her absence. It was nice to feel appreciated every now and then.

"Well, it'll be nice to have you around again, but don't push your-self. You hardly ever take a break anyway, might as well take as much time off as you can." Nina was quick to see through Iris' casually spoken words. She was concerned for Nina, for the recovery she most likely thought Nina would rush through—something Nina had been tempted to do, if she were to be honest. It made Nina feel a renewed fondness for her friend.

"Don't worry, I promise I'll only show back up at work when I'm perfectly fine."

"Good to know," Iris said, amusement clear in her voice.

She talked for a while longer with Iris, mostly about work and what Nina had been up to—which wasn't much, given that she was still trying to follow the doctor's instructions and rest. Iris didn't dwell on that subject, maybe because she felt that Nina wouldn't want to talk about it. Nina appreciated the gesture—and Iris herself—enough that she was sorry when the call ended and she was once more left with only the voices streaming from the television as company.

A game show was on, one that Nina hardly ever watched. She knew she wouldn't be paying much mind to it then and left it on, the sound of it all that mattered. With that, she walked over to the kitchen, intent on preparing something to eat. On her way, she passed a picture frame hanging on the wall.

It was a simple black frame with a picture of her and her mother shortly before the older woman passed away. Nina had just graduated college, was just barely a young adult about to head off into the world without any idea of what awaited her. At her side, her mother smiled with the barest hint of sadness at the thought of her daughter moving away. Nina almost regretted that.

The picture was one that had once been painful to look at but had become something Nina held dear. A simple, bittersweet memory captured in a second.

The light streaming from the windows reflected off the clear glass and, for a moment, Nina froze. A series of images flashed in her mind, a hallway with a picture hanging from it's cream colored walls—woods in autumn painted in warm shades against a grey sky—and the scent of spices lingering in the air. A soothing song played in the background, melancholy words sung in a foreign language. One moment the painting was in front of her, and the next Nina was standing in her apartment with the sounds of cheering coming from the television in the living room and the smell of petrichor still present around her. The smiling face of her mother gazed back at her through the glass.

The change was jarring, enough so that Nina felt a dull throbbing in her head. Disconcerted by what had just happened, she stood there, trying to figure out where the image had come from.

Before the accident—before the faint memories of heat and pain and the wailing of an ambulance in the distance—Nina had an impeccable memory. She was, after all, a journalist. A good one, with a mind perfect for retaining facts and details. That had all changed in an instant with the screeching of tires and the stifling sensation of being engulfed in flames and smoke. A burning pain inside and out, driving her into unconsciousness.

After that, Nina's mind had been a fractured mess, unable to preserve even the simplest of memories. Her long term memory was gone, according to doctors. Or at least, the ability to create long term memories was. Nina didn't know how she'd felt at that time—couldn't remember how she'd responded—but when she thought back to it, she couldn't help but be horrified.

The last memory she held could have been one of nothing but pain and fear.

The following months were a blank slate in her mind. She remembered waking up after the procedure, confused and with scars that she couldn't recall having gained. Nina recalled the explanation her doctors and her father had given her and the sense of panic at having lost so much time pulsing through her, leaving her a rattled mess.

Memory, she realized, was a strange but precious thing.

Nina didn't want to dwell on that any longer. Her life, she thought, was finally getting back on track. There was no need to linger on things she could no longer change or on the strange visions that plagued her as of late. It wasn't until later that her thoughts returned to her ever changing memories and mental state.

She was in bed, still caught between that odd stage between wakefulness and sleep. The sounds of the city seemed like a distant thing, even with only the glass of her window and the blinds covering it separating her from the outside world. Slowly, her consciousness slipped, trickling away towards a full slumber and just as she was on the cusp of it, the image of that now all too familiar hall appeared.

Nina could smell flowers—lavender, she thought. The scent subtle yet distinct as were the soft, almost delicate piano notes ringing in the hall. Something about it all seemed familiar, like a childhood home Nina had walked through time after time, despite her knowing otherwise. She could hear her own steps, sharp notes that clashed against the soothing atmosphere.

Just a few steps ahead, Nina could see something hanging from the wall. A picture frame, she thought at first, before realizing it was a mirror, framed in silver, glinting even in the soft lighting. Two steps away and Nina felt her hair brush against her cheek and fall over her shoulders.

One step away, and Nina had the distinct feeling that something was wrong.

She stood in front of the mirror only a second later. An unfamiliar face stared back at her through vibrant green eyes—so different from her own hazel ones—dark circles stood out starkly on the pale, freckled skin, almost giving it a sickly look. Chestnut hair fell around her face and over her thin shoulders while pink lips settled in a grim line.

Nina stared back at a stranger.

She awoke with a start, gasping for air and with a deep sense of confusion about what she'd just seen. Her heart beat wildly in her chest, drumming against her ears while her eyes flickered around the room. The time was 1:26 AM and Nina knew already that she would not be getting any more sleep that night.

Chapter 2

The scent of lavender hung in the air, a delicate fragrance that seemed comforting—familiar. A soft tune played in the background, wispy sounding notes ringing in Nina's ears contrasted with the sharp sound of her own steps. There was the glimmer of the mirror just a few steps away as Nina's heart pounded. The woman from the mirror finally had a name.

Two steps away and she felt a foreign sort of panic, distant yet still distinct. Her steps halted.

Green eyes stared back from a pale face—unwavering—and Nina knew it was wrong. Panic crept up, clawing at her throat in the form of a scream being muffled even as the placid look on the face that should have been Nina's stayed in place.

She awoke with a start, heart still beating wildly in her chest and hands shaking so very slightly. The clock showed the time as being just past five and Nina felt already exhausted. It was a feeling that persisted for the rest of the day.

Nina felt her whole body ache as she sat at her kitchen table some hours later, a cup of coffee in front of her. Steam rose from it, carrying the usual, earthy scent that had never failed to soothe Nina. Even so, at that time it did nothing to rid her of the unease she'd carried from the moment she'd woken up.

"Breaking news, this morning the commissioner of the FDA passed away in the hospital. . . ." The woman on the screen looked grim as she read the news. Nina only half listened, the voice sounding distant as her mind swam with thoughts of the oddness in her life.

Two days had passed since the dream. The one where Nina stared at a face that wasn't her own and felt like screaming from the wrongness of it all. Two days since visions of the strangely familiar hallway—with it's ever changing pictures hanging on the wall—began to interrupt Nina's daily life, wearing at Nina's already strained mind.

". . . No motive for the attack has been found. . . ."

Her once comfortable apartment felt stifling. Nina, for the first time since she'd moved into the city and occupied the brightly lit apartment, felt trapped in her own home. Perhaps that was why she felt an overwhelming sense of relief that surprised even herself when she received a message from a friend.

This time it was from Natalia—or Nat, as she preferred to be called—someone Nina had known since they were both children living in a smaller town. Simply seeing her name brought the image of the tall young woman to mind, her brown eyes as sharp as her smile. Nat was a clever woman, but she was also kind, and Nina found that made for a good combination in a friend.

It was, Nina thought, just the type of friend she needed at the moment. Maybe that was why she found herself smiling when she read Nat's message, asking if Nina would like to meet up. The timing couldn't have been better.

After sending a quick reply, Nina readied herself, thinking perhaps the fresh air and company would be of help. Perhaps for a short while, the hallway that had come to haunt her would leave her mind.

As soon as she stepped out of the building, Nina felt like a weight was lifted off her shoulders; swept away in the cool, late autumn breeze. She took a deep breath of the crisp air, took a look around at the scene of people simply going about their business all around her, and went on her way.

The place where she was to meet Nat was a short walk away. Normally, Nina would have driven there, but she needed some time to get out of the shaky frame of mind she'd been in as of late. Taking a walk always helped her clear her head, and at that moment, she found that simply being surrounded by others walking along that same street helped.

By the time Nina reached the coffee shop where Nat waited for her, she was feeling more like herself—or at least, like her old self. That was something that had become rare after the accident and the surgery. Nina liked to think it was simply because she was still recovering. She liked to think that things would get better.

Despite that, some part of her must have known the things she'd gone through had changed her too much.

The bells on the coffee shop door jingled daintily when Nina walked into the cozy little store. There were not so many people waiting around, perhaps because of the odd hour—too late for breakfast and too early for lunch. Nina was glad for that much.

Nat sat at a table off to the side, next to the window where she could watch people walk by and go about their business. She looked much like she had the last time Nina had seen her, something that must have been more than a month back. They were both busy people, after all.

Nat's long, dark hair was neatly clipped back and a thoughtful expression was on her face, making her look as if she was caught in her own thoughts. Even so, her eyes still held a keen sort of look that Nina had come to associate so closely to her friend. Of course, Nat's eyes had always stood out to Nina for more than one reason.

When Nat finally saw Nina, she smiled, crimson lips curving across her pale face as she stood to greet Nina with a hug. Her warmth was comforting, despite Nina's usual dislike of physical affection. She supposed, at times, a bit of it was needed—maybe even appreciated. The embrace was quick, Nat drawing back to look at Nina, seemingly appraising her friend's condition.

"How have you been?" Nat asked, voice soft and just faintly tinged with concern.

"I'm fine," Nina said, feeling as if that were true at that moment. "Tired, but fine. I guess it's just taking some getting used to not remembering so much."

"I bet it does." Nat took her seat once more as Nina sat across from her. She noticed a warm drink already waiting for her. "Oh, I ordered something for you. Figured you'd need something to warm you up with this weather."

Nina smiled at the gesture and took a sip of the drink Nat had ordered for her. It was sweet, a bit too much so for her taste, but she still smiled as she set her cup down.

"Thank you," she said, the taste of cream and sugar still stuck to her mouth. Nat smiled, pleased. "How has work been for you?"

"Busy, like always. The company's expanding and we might be moving to a new location soon, but I won't bore you with the details." Nat waved the issue away with a simple gesture of her hand. "By the way, I'm sorry I couldn't visit you before, things have just been so busy and then I wasn't sure how you were doing."

"It's fine, I understand. We all have our own lives. I'm just glad we could meet up now, it's a nice change from being stuck at home all the time." Nina smiled at her friend in what she hoped was a comforting manner.

"Yeah, well, I didn't want to bother you before you were well enough. You look good," Nat commented, lifting her cup to her lips, steam still rising from the drink.

Nina supposed she did, considering all she had been through. The mention of it—the very thought of it—still made her all the more conscious of the burns that were still healing. Skin grafting could only do so much and Nina knew she'd have scars left over to remind her of the accident. Constant reminders of what had happened. Subconsciously, she tugged at the sleeve of her sweater beneath the table.

"I feel good, it's just odd sometimes," Nina said, halting before she said anything about the real issues she had been dealing with. Unfortunately for Nina, Nat was a very perceptive person. Her brown eyes seemed to look through her, the mismatched tones—something Nat claimed only Nina had ever been able to notice so quickly—unsettling for the first time since Nina had first gazed at them so many years earlier.

"Is something wrong?" Nat asked, brow furrowed

Nina hesitated for a moment, mulling over whether she should tell Nat. She was well aware of how ridiculous what she was going through sounded. Still, Nat was someone she could trust, someone she had known for a very long time. There were few people Nina could trust to the same level as she did Nat.

"It's just, lately I've been having these strange dreams," Nina started, still feeling uncertain but needing to tell someone. Nat looked interested, her left eye—the one that had been replaced—seeming to glimmer even in the soft lighting of the shop.

"What kind of dreams? About the accident?"

Nina shook her head. "No, they're not really about that. Honestly, I don't know what they're about. I don't even know if they're really dreams anymore."

The last part seemed to pique Nat's interest. She sat up straighter, hand drifting away from her drink and gaze fixed unwaveringly on her friend. Nina chose to take that as a sign that she should continue. She struggled for a second, thinking of how best to describe her issue.

How best to tell her friend that she thought she was losing her mind.

"When you had the accident, did you have any strange side effects?" Nina began, hesitant to ask about the event that had cost Nat her eye, but needing to get a better understanding on what was going on. Nat seemed surprised, something Nina expected. She was glad to note that she didn't also look offended.

"It took some getting used to," Nat said nonchalantly, fingers idly stirring her coffee. "There was some sensitivity to light the first few weeks, headaches, trouble focusing my vision. Little things. Now a days I don't even think about it so much. If I strain my sight too much the headaches might come back, but everything else is fine. Sometimes I can almost forget the whole thing ever happened. Why? Are you having issues?" Nina nodded.

"Nothing serious. The headaches are fading, but those I expected," she said. "But the dreams. I didn't expect those."

"It's not unheard of to have strange dreams after something like what you've gone through."

"No, it isn't," Nina agreed, because she'd seen it before. People who'd gone through traumatic experiences often found little respite in their sleep. "At first I thought it was normal, with everything that's happened. I thought maybe it had to do with the time between the accident and the surgery."

"The period of time you don't remember," Nat said, nodding in understanding.

"Yes, but that can't be it. Those memories are gone, so I know it's something else. But I still have no idea what it's all about. There's places I know I've never been to, and they just keep popping up in my head like triggered memories, and they're so vivid," there was a trace of desperation in Nina's voice that she recognized all on her own. Nat appeared to do so as well, if the expression of gradually growing concern she wore was anything to go by.

"Maybe you should talk to the doctors, see what they have to say about it. It is a new procedure, there's bound to be things even they don't know about, or maybe things they forgot to mention."

Nina had considered that, had hoped that was all it was, but she knew there were others who'd received hippocampal implants before her and had not reported such strange side effects. Still, she'd said enough. She didn't want to worry Nat any more than she already had.

Mostly, Nina didn't think she should mention the woman in the mirror.

They left not long after, Nat wearing a smile that Nina was certain was meant to be reassuring. She found no comfort in it, but still put on a smile of her own. Nat gave her one last hug before walking away. Nina watcher her go until she was lost in the crowd. The sickly sweet taste of the coffee Nat had ordered for her stuck to Nina's mouth and she found her mind wasn't any clearer than it had been at the start.

Nina was just glad to make it back to her home without the image of the hallway returning to her mind. She was still tired, the exhaustion appearing to reach her very bones. That was how she ended up laying on her living room couch just shortly after arriving. The television was instantly turned on at her command. As was usual for Nina as of late, she had no real interest in the programs currently playing, but the sound served to cut through the overwhelming silence of the apartment. Distracted her from recalling the unsettling silence of the hospital room she'd woken up in all those weeks earlier.

"... is currently awaiting sentencing. . . ."

The conversation she'd had with Nat replayed in her head. For a second, Nina found herself wondering whether her friend was right, whether she should simply go back to the research center and ask about the strange memory-like visions that were plaguing her. That was, after all, the most reasonable course of action she could take. If anyone could tell her what was wrong, it was the doctors who'd treated her. Nina might have done that, if it weren't for some part of her pushing her away from that, telling her that she shouldn't go back—not yet. Nina's instincts had yet to give her a reason to doubt them.

"... Fearnley was indicted on the murder of Alice Cassill. . . ."

Nina sat up on the couch, intending to head to the kitchen to start on a somewhat late lunch. Perhaps that would help rid her of the remnants of the overly sweet drink she'd had not so long ago. Her gaze swept across the television screen as she turned towards the kitchen. And then, Nina froze.

There, on the screen, was the face that had haunted her for the last couple of days. Green eyes stared back from a pale face, dark circles giving the otherwise young woman a tired look. Nina felt like screaming—felt like the world around her had fallen away in that instant.

Chapter 3

Alice Cassill—a name that swam in Nina's mind from the moment she'd seen the picture that accompanied it. Her green eyes were brought to the forefront of Nina's mind every time the name occurred to her. It was the impassive gaze of a dead woman—the thought alone sent a chill down Nina's spine.

She'd been shocked at first, barely registering whatever it was that the newscaster was talking about. By the time Nina was able to focus, it was too late. The reporter moved on to a different story and Nina was left wanting for answers. For a while, she sat there, staring in shock at the screen without truly seeing the images playing across it. Her mind was whirring with all sort of thoughts, some more morbid than others. None of them were reassuring.

Once Nina managed to calm herself, one thing was clear—she needed answers.

"...Is rumored to be the top pick for the new Commissioner of the FDA...."

Despite the myriad of feelings still swirling inside of her, she knew she needed to find out more about the woman named Alice. Nina sat there, gathering herself. By the time she stood from the couch, she had convinced herself that it was all just another story. One more article she needed to research. The thought served to calm her for only as long as she didn't think about it too deeply.

After that, Nina merely followed her instincts as a journalist. She sat at her desk, the news having ended long ago and a new show playing on the television, with the voices streaming over to her as only a faint series of murmurs that were largely ignored. Dinner time had come and gone with Nina hardly feeling even the smallest pang of hunger. The exhaustion she'd felt from the painfully early start of her day was momentarily forgotten. It was swept away by Nina's thirst for answers.

Alice was not a difficult woman to find information on. She was a prominent researcher, despite her young age. The woman was a scientist, specializing in neuroscience. Nina was only mildly surprised to learn that Alice worked at the research center where Nina had sought treatment. After all, the place was the largest of its kind in the area and renowned for having some of the best specialists in their respective fields.

What came as a shock was the knowledge that Alice had also been working on neural prosthetics before her death. More specifically, she'd been working on hippocampal implants.

Nina felt her mouth go dry as she read over the information, her eyes staring at the words displayed on the overly bright screen.

Something inside her, some instinct she had developed after years of working as an investigative journalist, told her that was it—that was a key detail in the mess that her life had become after the accident. It was something that was necessary if she wanted to understand what was going on with her mind.

Still, that didn't explain why it was Alice that occupied the mirror in her dreams. Nina sat back in her chair, once more feeling the exhaustion of the day after what seemed like hours of managing to ignore it. Her back ached nearly as much as her head, a dull throbbing building up and making her close her eyes in an attempt to quell the pain as it slowly increased.

Against her will, her mind slowly wandered away from thoughts of Alice, drifting off with Nina hardly noticing.

And then, she was standing in the hall once more. The polished hardwood floors and cream colored walls looked the same as always, the lighting warm and soft—almost inviting. As always, Nina moved calmly down the hall, the sound of her steps sharp, nearly too loud in the sparsely furnished space. A melody, different from the past ones, rang in the air. It was the sound of strings accompanied by piano notes that set a steady tempo. There was the scent of wet earth and damp wood, vivid enough that Nina could nearly picture it.

Just ahead of her, the familiar frame hung on the wall. Despite her calm movements, there was a spark of panic in Nina's mind at the thought that she might just see a face that didn't belong to her. The sense of wrongness returned as it always did, something that didn't belong to that memory, Nina knew.

To her great relief, it was not a pair of green eyes that stared back at her when she reached the frame. Instead, Nina found a painting. Warm hues of red, orange and bright yellow brought to life the woods surrounding a sparkling river beneath a hazy blue sky. Nina stared at the picture through a stranger's eyes, studying each vivid detail.

And then, there was a break in the patter of Nina's usual dreams. A hand that was not her own, pale and thin, reached out to the picture. A slim finger pointed at a spot in the painting. It was a small thing, nearly hidden in the back and obscured by the brightly colored details surrounding it, but Nina saw it all the same. There, beneath the brightly colored leaves, was a bridge.

At that moment, Nina awoke, still sitting on her chair. The harsh light from the computer in front of her hurt her eyes, while the darkness that had settled around her felt oppressive, the room feeling colder than it should have. Nina ignored it all along with the rapid beating of her heart. Instead, she pulled out a notepad from a drawer of her desk and hurried to note as much of her dream as she could recall with a slightly shaking hand.

The details, she knew, were likely to fade over time, and something told her they mattered too much to be allowed to leave her mind. Nina's mind might have been fractured, her memories a mess that she was still trying to repair, but she knew there was work that needed to be done. With as much detail as she could recall, Nina jotted down all of the visions of the hallway she'd had. The scents, sounds, and pictures were ever changing and Nina knew there was something there that she wasn't seeing. Something in all those images that made them so vivid.

"Almost like a memory," she muttered thoughtfully, pen halting with the tip hovering right above the paper as the realization hit Nina.

She was looking through Alice's eyes, after all. In every single of the so-called visions, Nina had been but a spectator looking through those green eyes that had come to haunt her. It was so obvious that Nina wondered how she hadn't seen it before. But how?

Nina supposed that it could be possible. After all, the very implant that she'd received had once been considered an impossibility. The science behind memories was a complex one, but it was advancing. It wasn't unreasonable to think that a way to truly implant someone's memories into another would someday be possible. Nina had just never thought it would be so soon.

". . . Fearnley's trial for the slaying of Alice Cassill is set for November 21st. . . ."

Nina's thoughts shifted—the newfound revelation of what those visions and dreams really were pushed back for the time being—the sounds from the television in the living room carried over and the name of the woman from her dreams claimed her attention. This time, though, there was another name that stood out. All on their own, Nina's feet led her back to the living room, where she stood and watched the now painfully familiar image of Alice on the screen for a second before the news anchor moved on to another story.

"Fearnley," Nina said in a near whisper, back to ignoring what the woman narrating the daily news was saying.

Nina set aside the notebook and turned back to her computer, fingers deftly moving across the keyboard. A moment later, she was looking at a picture of Christopher Fearnley on the screen. He was thin, pale, and with a look of total exhaustion in his blue eyes that was all too clear even in a photograph.

Fearnley, she knew, was accused of killing Alice in her home, but the details of the crime were still a mystery to Nina. As she read about the crime the man was said to have committed, there was one thing that Nina couldn't help but think was missing. For all the coverage Fearnley had received, his motives remained as unclear as they'd been on the day he was arrested.

Maybe it was because he'd confessed, or maybe it was because the image Nina had of Fearnley from what she'd learned of the man didn't match up with the crime.

The man who'd taken Alice's life was about as average as anyone else. He was a mild looking middle-aged man with a job at an electronics company and not even so much as a parking ticket on his record. His wife had divorced him years earlier and there was no mention of any later relations. Not a single detail stood out to Nina, despite a part of her saying that there had to be something else, something she wasn't seeing. Still, by all accounts, he was the last person one would suspect of murder. But there it was, on every article Nina had read—Fearnley had confessed.

"... New studies find that the treatment could potentially be used to help those with psychological disorders. ...." The news anchor looked steadily at the camera, her expression impassive. It was unsettlingly reminiscent of Alice's face staring back through the mirror. Enough so that Nina changed the channel without truly thinking about it.

The news anchor disappeared, replaced by a stern faced man. Nina recognized the movie playing as one of murders, spies and conspiracies the likes of which Nina had never thought she would be involved in. She nearly laughed at how wild her life had turned out, even without the conspiracy theories and other nonsense. The only thing holding her back was the migraine that was just starting to fade and the feeling of being trapped in a life that no longer seemed like her own.

Instead Nina yawned and looked at the time, near midnight. She'd been sitting at her desk for hours, searching for information in a nearly obsessive way. The start of the day seemed like a distant thing. The memory of cloyingly sweet coffee coating her mouth and Nat sitting across from her with a crimson smile and mismatched eyes felt like too simple a memory for a life as complicated as Nina's currently was.

Slowly, Nina stood, her back protesting the movement after having spent so long sitting. Her head ached only the slightest bit, the pain faint enough so that Nina could ignore it in favor of getting some rest. Sleep came easy to her that night, more so than Nina had expected. She found herself falling asleep quickly and suddenly instead of the gradual shift that was so usual for her. One minute she was staring up at the ceiling and the next she was once again standing in the hallway.

Against her will, Nina found herself walking down the hall. The sound of her steps seemed deafening in the uncharacteristic silence. No song was playing, the only sounds those of Nina moving down the hall, heels clicking against the floor, and her soft breathing. There was a scent that seemed familiar, though nothing as soothing as the jasmine and spices that had wafted through the air the last time she'd found herself walking down that particular hall. This was a harsher smell, the memory of what it could be just out of reach of Nina's mind.

Before she could think of what it could be, she found herself standing before the mirror. Alice's face stared back, as impassive as ever—pale and sickly looking. Even then, her green eyes blazed with what Nina thought could only be unflinching determination. Something, however, was different this time. On top of the casual shirt Alice had worn every other time, there was a lab coat of a pristine white color. The change stood out to Nina immediately.

Alice gazed back into the mirror, unmoving, for a second. Then, she raised her hand and, with a single finger, tapped a rectangular nametag on the lab coat. There was no name on it, nothing but the name of the research center where Alice worked: SEIN.

Nina awoke a moment later, puzzled as always by the strange visions of Alice in that silver mirror. Without a moment's thought, Nina got up, intending to note down as much of the dream as she could recall. Her covers were tossed to the side, and her bare feet slapped against the floor as she moved to her desk and searched for her notebook. She did not intend to get any more sleep that night.

It was just past five and Nina had much to do.

Chapter 4

The prison was as austere a place as one would expect. Nina, despite all the times she'd had to step inside the place for the various articles that demanded it, never quite got used to the feeling being inside the building invoked. Still, it was a necessity—one that had forced her to call in a few favors to accomplish without having to wait for approval—and Nina had become accustomed to doing things she didn't particularly like for the sake of the truth.

All of the details were still clear in her mind, and Nina focused on keeping a firm grasp of them as she worked. The phone on her coffee table went ignored, the message that had been left would have to wait.

The truth she was after that day was perhaps the most important of all.

She sat in the cold, metal seat she'd been provided and waited, with only the sound of the clock on the wall ticking away keeping her company. A cup of coffee sat on the metal table in front of her, black and still steaming. The scent it let out was the most inviting thing she'd come across in that miserable place. The taste of it was bitter, earthy—it helped to calm her nerves.

Nina had only to wait a short time before the door opened with a faint creaking sound and then the man she was there to speak to walked in followed by a guard.

Christopher Fearnley was as average a man as Nina had first thought he'd be when she'd seen his face displayed on her computer screen and then splashed across her television every time the news was on. He was shorter than her—though she was a tall woman—with mousy hair that was already graying, particularly around the sides, and eyes of a washed out blue tone. Dark circles gave him a sickly look as they contrasted with the paleness of his skin and the corners of his thin lips were tilted down into the slightest of frowns. Fearnley looked painfully pale beneath the harsh lighting of the room. The clothes he'd been issued seemed to hang off him, and Nina recalled that he hadn't looked so thin in the pictures she'd seen. The stress of it all must have taken a toll on him even in the short time he'd been imprisoned—Nina couldn't blame him.

The guard who'd lead him in cuffed him to the table and walked out without uttering so much as a single word. Nina sat there for a second, observing Fearnley. His gaze remained pointed down at the table, the paper cup of water within his reach went ignored.

"Thank you for meeting with me, Mr. Fearnley," Nina said, her voice taking on the same tone she used when she interviewed people. It was professional—cool and calm enough to seem cordial while keeping a distance between Nina and whoever she was speaking to.

Fearnley didn't respond.

"I'm Nina Sheppard with—"

"I know who you are, the guards told me. Why are you here, Ms. Sheppard," Fearnley cut Nina off. His voice was calm, tired, and softer than Nina had expected. It fit the mild mannered looking man sitting across from her. "I've confessed already. What else would you need to know?"

It took Nina a moment to gather her thoughts and formulate an answer.

"I'm here because there's something that hasn't been made clear."

"You want to know why I did it," Fearnley said, mouth twisting into a frustrated sort of grimace for a second. "It's what everyone wants to know. The only thing they all care about."

"Motive is always important in a case," Nina said, reciting words she'd heard time and again through her career.

"A mad man doesn't need a motive. That's what the guards say anyway."

"You hardly look mad to me." Nina had seen her share of mad men in her life, had reported on many of them. Fearnley looked stressed—on the brink of breaking—but still sane enough to look positively haunted by his current predicament as he sat across from her. Still holding together well enough to be tired of the constant questions and therefore, to be wary of Nina.

Still, she hadn't expected it to be so simple. It had been enough of a risk to bring up the reason for her visit so early into their meeting. Under different circumstances, Nina might not have done so, but on that day, time was not on her side. If she wanted to find out what had driven Fearnley to kill Alice she'd have to learn more about the man. Up on the wall, the clock continued to tick away.

"Mr. Fearnley, how did you know Alice Cassill?" she asked, hoping for an actual answer. Fearnley hesitated for a moment. He shifted in his seat, eyes flicking up to Nina for a second before diverting back down to the table.

"She worked at the research center where I was being treated, SEIN" Fearnley said after a while. The acronym for the South East Institute of Neuroprosthetics was something Nina was already familiar with. "Worked with neuroprosthetics."

"What kind of treatment did you receive there?" Fearnley was surprised by the question. No one had asked him that before, Nina realized.

"I got an implant, something to help my memory."

Now it was Nina's turn to be thrown off. She wasn't sure what sort of expression was displayed on her face, but it was enough to make Fearnley look at her strangely.

"A hippocampal implant?" Fearnley nodded.

"Yeah, a couple months back I got into an accident at work. Couldn't remember a thing after that. Heard of this new treatment and I must have figured there was nothing to lose. Next thing I know, I'm waking up on a hospital bed with the worst headache of my life and two and a half months have passed."

"Must have been difficult," Nina said. Belatedly, she realized her tone had slipped away from the even, professional voice she'd been using. The words had sounded just the slightest bit softer, sympathy poorly hidden within them.

"It was, but I was just glad it worked." Fearnley shrugged, the chain of the handcuffs jingling with the movement.

"Did you see Dr.Cassill often?"

"I guess. I had to keep going back for checkups, she'd see me sometimes. Doctors said I was doing just fine. Guess something must have gone wrong after all."

"Why do you say that?"

Fearnley seemed to think about how best to answer. Nina resisted the urge to look at the time, knowing all too well she was running out of it.

"To be honest, I don't really remember what happened all that well," Fearnley said after a minute. Despite the vague answer, Nina knew he was talking about Alice. "The memories are there, but they're not all clear. Could be because I'd just gotten fixed up."

"But you confessed," Nina said, wondering how someone could admit to committing a crime without having a clear recollection of the event.

"Because I did it," Fearnley said, with enough conviction that Nina stopped short. "I remember that much." The words were spoken quietly, with regret and guilt that should have told anyone there was more to the story. It made Nina wonder just what Fearnley remembered about that night.

Before Nina could ask Fearnley anything else, her time was up. There was a series of knocks on the door before the same guard entered the room.

"If you ever want to talk more," Nina said, handing Fearnley a piece of paper with her name and number she'd prepared ahead of time. He didn't answer, but he took the slip of paper. Nina figured that had to be enough.

The guard took Fearnley away. The man said not a word as he was led out, shoulders hunched and eyes fixed on the ground, hand still clasping Nina's phone number. Nina walked out into the sunlight and cool autumn air not long after.

She went over the conversation she'd had with Fearnley, over the little she'd learned about his relationship with Alice. If it could even be called that. The truth was, Nina was still no closer to figuring out what was going on.

Fearnley's motive was still unclear. As far as she could see he'd hardly known Alice, and yet he himself was certain of his own guilt. Alice herself was still a mystery—one that Nina had to solve if she had any hopes of understanding what was going on in her own head. With that thought in mind, Nina made her way to her car. There was still a lot she needed to do.

As the day turned to night, Nina sat in her living room. All of the files that she was able to gather on Fearnley and Alice—which weren't as many as she'd like—were strewn around her, both on the couch and on the coffee table in front of her. A plate of half eaten food sat on the corner of said table along with a pair of empty mugs that had once held coffee. The television screen displayed the smiling face of a woman enjoying a day at the beach as a voiceover listed the side effects for some new drug.

Nina stared not at the screen, but at the pages she'd gone over more than once, trying to see what she was missing—attempting to find the connection between the two people and the memories that continued to play in her mind at the slightest trigger. Nina knew it was still a long shot. Knew that anyone else would have taken Nat's suggestion to see a doctor. At the very least, most people would have seen Fearnley and Alice's connection as irrelevant to the issue at hand. Still, there was something telling Nina that she needed to know what happened. She needed to find out why Fearnley had killed Alice.

Learning that the man had connections to the same research center where Nina had been treated—where Alice had worked—had only made Nina that much more determined to find out the truth. Especially with the knowledge that Fearnley had also received the same kind of implant as Nina. Some part of her couldn't help but feel sympathetic. After all, Nina was all too familiar with the feeling of trying to put things back together without having all the pieces. That was what it had always felt like to Nina, from the moment she'd awoken after her surgery months after the accident.

Then, just as she thought things were getting better, the visions she was now almost certain were Alice's memories started up. Her unreadable expression as she stared back at Nina was a thought that kept crossing Nina's mind.

What if it crossed Fearnley's mind too, Nina thought, the idea coming to her suddenly. What if Fearnley had those same memories as me. But why wouldn't he tell anyone?

As soon as the last thought occurred to her Nina knew the answer. Even she'd had trouble telling anyone—even those she trusted, like Nat and Iris—about the things she was seeing. Why would Fearnley ever confide in someone he didn't know. And then there was the question of why.

Why would Alice ever do something like that to the people in her care? Even if she were able to do such a thing, Nina couldn't figure out why she would implant a series of nonsensical memories into someone she didn't know.

Nina's tired eyes swept over the mess on her table only to stop on the worn notebook where she'd been jotting down every single memory of the hall and the pictures.Every scent, every sound and every single picture had been written down as soon as Nina's mind had returned to reality. She'd yet to find a pattern that could provide her an answer, perhaps because there was still so much she didn't know about Alice and her circumstances.

A yawn left Nina's mouth, her tired eyes closing as her mouth opened. She knew she needed to sleep when the simple task of opening her eyes felt all too difficult. Her eyelids felt heavy, too heavy to stay up for much longer. Slowly, Nina drifted off to sleep on her couch. The people on the television chattered on as the light of the screen washed over Nina's sleeping form.

She was aware of none of this as she was transported back to that cream colored wall with the hardwood floors. Her feet, as they always did, moved on their own with each step echoing along the hall. Other than that, there was no sound. No faintly playing music or almost lonely sounding singing, just Nina's steps and the near silent sound of her steady breaths. The lighting seemed brighter somehow, livelier, and her steps were just a tad quicker than usual.

Nina could still see the frame at the end of the hall, just a few more steps and she would stand before it. And then, she was there, and from the corner of her eye Nina saw the picture frame as she walked by it without so much as a moment's pause. Her hand rose, looking strangely small, and clasped around a plain door knob painted gold. She felt the knob turn, saw a sliver of bright sunlight pour out as the door opened.

Nina woke up to the sound of an early morning show playing on the television and her phone vibrating against the top of her coffee table. It took her a moment to realize where she was, the walls of the hallway gone too suddenly and her mind still struggling to keep up with things. It was only a moment later that she registered just how different her dream had been from the others. Almost automatically, Nina reached for her notebook, intending to write down as much as she could recall.

Chapter 5

The picture depicted a vineyard painted in brilliant greens and earthy browns. Pink, red, yellow, and orange tones blended into a perfect sunset. In Nina's mind, the image faded, replaced by a more familiar one. There was no scent of jasmine or spices. No faint music playing somewhere nearby. No hallway with cream colored walls or the clacking of shoes on hardwood floors. No green eyes staring intently back at Nina. The short bit of normalcy Nina had achieved seemed already like a distant memory

Just the autumn woods and the river. It was there for a second and gone in the next. Once it was gone, Nina felt a chill run through her.

For that one small moment in which the painting of the forest flashed through her mind, Nina thought of it as nothing more than a recollection pulled from her own memories. It made her wonder just how deeply ingrained in her mind Alice's memories were.

The thought was a fleeting one, but it was enough to disturb Nina. With a shaking hand, she raised her cup to her mouth and took a sip of the hot drink. It was a bit of normalcy—just a cup of coffee in a cozy shop—but it helped to ground Nina. She still avoided looking back at the painting on the wall.

When someone finally approached her table, Nina thought it a welcome distraction. She smiled faintly, hoping any unease she still felt was properly hidden, and looked up at the man who she'd agreed to meet there.

He smiled at Nina as he took a seat, dimples appearing as his lips curved up and brown eyes sparkling.

"You're late," Nina said, setting her cup down and not sounding the least bit reproachful. She'd long ago learned not to rely on Ben's poor time management abilities.

"Sorry, traffic was a nightmare," he said, sounding just the slightest bit frustrated, but his eyes lighting up at the drink that waited in front of him. "Makes me wonder why I ever moved to the city."

Nina's lips quirked up just the slightest bit at the usual complaint. Benjamin Valle was an easy going man on most accounts, but big city traffic would forever be his pet peeve. It was something Nina had learned well enough in the year they'd dated. Still, he was a good man, a good friend—something few could say about their ex. He hummed appreciatively when he tasted his drink. Nina might have forgotten many things, but she still remembered how Ben—an avid lover of coffee—liked his daily caffeine fix.

"How've you been doing?" he asked, eyes flickering from Nina's eyes to the scar just barely visible as it peeked out from Nina's sweater. She made a very conscious effort not to tug at her sleeve of hide her hand beneath the table. "You know, I meant to visit at the hospital. Figured it might not be the best time though."

"It's fine, wouldn't have mattered anyway. I can't even remember anything that happened while I was there." That knowledge might have still bothered Nina, but she knew she had to get used to the idea if she wanted to get over it.

"Maybe it's for the best. Things have really been going to shit lately," Ben said with a shrug.

"I take it work's been rough."

"Pretty much. Everyone at work's going crazy over the Commissioner of the FDA and then we have a whole series of burglaries lately that we're looking into." Ben sighed, leaning back in his seat. Nina had almost forgotten just how demanding Ben's work could be. How much of a toll being an officer took on him, despite him not wanting to admit it. "Then there's the protests. Been a pain with everyone arguing 'bout the memory implant thing."

"Memory implant?" Nina asked, nearly spilling her coffee as she'd been about to pick it up.

"Yeah, some doctors want to try treating people with implanted memories. They think it could help with therapy. Some people have been complaining, saying it's not ethical. Can't say they're wrong." Ben shrugged and sipped his drink.

"I thought they already did that." It was then that Nina recalled reading about it once. She was sure one of her colleagues had written about the topic. "Isn't it really just hypnosis?"

"Not this type. They actually make false memories and stick them into people. Apparently that's supposed to help them sort things out. Honestly, that'd just give me more issues."

"Have they done any human testing?"

"Don't know, didn't really pay much attention to the news when it came up. Probably haven't. I think they were asking the FDA for authorization." Ben looked up from his drink, something in his expression—so relaxed, though tired—shifted in that moment. "But I didn't call you to talk about depressing stuff. No wonder you dumped me," Ben joked, attempting to lighten the mood. Nina couldn't help but smile a bit.

"I thought it was mutual."

"We mutually agreed for you to dump me." Nina found herself laughing for what felt like the first time in a long while. She didn't notice the satisfied smile on Ben's face at the small accomplishment.

"What we both agreed on was that we were both workaholics," she said after a minute, smile still in place. For that moment, all thoughts of Alice and the memories that weren't Nina's own were pushed to the back. It was a moment of normalcy Nina could appreciate.

The moment was shattered by a sharp pain shooting through Nina's head. It was bad enough that it made her wince and lift a hand to her head. Ben's playful demeanor slipped away in an instant, concern overtaking him as he leaned closer to Nina.

"What's wrong?" he asked.

As quickly as it had come, the pain began to ebb away until it was nothing more than a minor annoyance. Nina sat up, her hand returning to the table, next to her coffee.

"It's nothing, I've just been getting headaches. Probably because of the implant," she said, attempting to put Ben at ease. She didn't mention that they had never been so sudden, or so strong.

"Maybe you should get that looked at." Ben frowned, brow furrowing as he studied Nina. "Have you been back for any check-ups?"

"Not lately, but they kept me at the hospital for a while. The doctor mentioned I might have some headaches for some time after the procedure and they're not as frequent lately."

Ben didn't seem to be completely at ease, but he could tell that Nina didn't want to talk about her health issues. She was already much too aware of them as it was. There was a moment of silence, both of them stuck in their own thoughts, before Nina broke it.

"Hey, did you hear about the researcher that was killed recently?" she asked, knowing there was a good chance that Ben would have some useful information.

"And here I thought I was the one with the morbid interests," Ben said. "Is that how you start a casual conversation?"

"Only with you," Nina shot back. Ben actually snorted at that before leaning back with a sigh.

"Yeah, I heard about that. Why?"

"She worked at the research center where I was treated," Nina said, doing her best to sound casual. "From what I hear, she also worked with neuroprosthetics. Might have treated me, for all I know." Ben grimaced, but still answered Nina's question.

"To be honest, I haven't been involved with that case all that much so I don't know much more than what's on the news."

Nina resisted the urge to frown. She'd been hoping Ben would have more knowledge about the case. Still, maybe there was something she could get out of him.

"Fearnley, right? That's the man who did it." Ben nodded. "Did they ever say why he killed her?"

Ben seemed to mull this question over, taking his time as he took a long drink from his coffee. Finally, he looked up at Nina.

"There's no clear motive. Not yet, at least." He paused and looked at Nina suspiciously. "You're not using me to get details for a story again, are you?" Nina would have felt insulted if she hadn't done precisely what Ben accused her of several times before.

"No! I'm not even back at work yet. Thinking of extending my leave if these headaches don't stop by the end of the week." Ben seemed to be convinced. Nina had always lied best when she told half truths. "So the guy just snapped and killed the doctor?"

"I guess. We don't really know, he hasn't said why he did it. Only thing we know is that he was a patient at the place where the victim worked. Maybe something happened at his last checkup." Ben shrugged, and Nina knew she wouldn't get much else out of him.

They finished their drinks and walked out together, standing in the cold and both looking just the slightest bit better than when they'd walked in.

"We should do this more often," Ben said, lips quirking up in a half smile.

"What, talk about depressing shit over barely decent coffee?"

"Yeah, nicer than talking about depressing shit over crappy coffee at work." Nina had to give him that much. "But seriously, if you ever want to talk or if you need anything just call me."

Nina felt a newfound appreciation for her friends when she thought of how open they had all been to helping her through such a difficult time. She just wished the problems she faced were mundane enough that she could rely on them. Instead, she had to hide behind a smile and reassure them that she was fine.

"Thanks," she said, feeling true gratitude. "I'm sure I'll be alright, but I'll call you sometime." Ben seemed to have expected that answer, going by the slightly exasperated look on his face.

"Sure, when you want the inside scoop on your next story." There was no real reproach there, just a show of how well Ben had gotten to know Nina. He was already turning to walk away, lips fixed in a small smile and hands tucked into his coat's pockets.

Nina watched him walk away before turning and heading off back to her apartment. Thoughts of Alice and Fearnley returning to her mind at once with Ben's departure. A headache was starting up already, building up little by little so that Nina had no doubt she'd feel the full force of it by the time she got home.

Chapter 6

The address on Nina's phone matched the place she stood before at that moment. Still, Nina could hardly picture Fearnley living in the rundown building where she'd just arrived. He'd seemed like a neat, nearly timid man when she'd spoken to him in prison. Then again, there was much she didn't know about the man.

Appearances could be deceiving. That was one of the many things her profession had taught her over the years.

With that in mind, Nina walked into the building with no one to question her. The inside was marginally better than the outside. There was no peeling paint on the walls or badly drawn graffiti. Just plain off-white walls and cheap linoleum on the halls. The place had an old feeling. It made Nina think of the place where she'd lived when she was very young.

Back when she was no more than three and her parents were still getting used to their new life of being married with a child. They'd shared a small apartment on top of a shop—a beauty salon, she thought it was—with a threadbare carpet and a similar type of cheap linoleum as the one in Fearnley's building making up the kitchen floor. It was small, nearly cramped, but Nina had some good memories there. Back then, life had been simpler and her parents had been happy. Back then, she'd had her mother.

Nina tried not to dwell on that as she climbed the stairs, wary as the steps creaked with each one of the steps she took. It was cold inside the building, nearly as cold as it was outside and Nina found herself pulling her coat closer around her.

Fearnley lived on the top floor—the third one—and Nina made it there without running into so much as another soul. For a second, she found herself questioning whether anyone else even lived in that building, but she knew they did, had heard the faint sounds of people talking from behind closed doors. Even as she reached the third floor, Nina thought she heard people arguing somewhere in the building and told herself it was just a television set too loudly.

Nina tried to focus on what she was there to do, especially once she took that first step down the hall and felt as if the walls were closing in around her. For a brief moment, she thought she could smell jasmine and spice, thought she could hear a piano playing nearby and feel chestnut hair slipping over her shoulder.

The end of the hall grew closer and closer, the clacking of Nina's steps too loud for her own ears. A mirror waited at the end, Nina just knew.

And then, she was standing before a black door with a number in peeling gold letters on it. No green eyes stared back at her and Nina almost felt silly for having thought they would. The relief she felt seemed like a tidal wave washing over her, leaving only the cold realization of just how deeply Alice's memories seemed to have invaded her mind. She shook those thoughts out of her mind, at least for as long as she could, and attempted to stay in the moment.

With one last look around her to make sure no one was watching her, Nina got to work.

Maybe she should have felt guiltier than she did for what she was about to do, or maybe she should have known it was wrong and given up even before she'd shown up to that old apartment building. Still, she told herself it was important, that it was the only reason she was there. She told herself that for as long as it took to pick the scratched up lock of Fearnley's door.

The short time the task took felt like hours. Every sound was amplified, ever whisper of wind seeming like the breath of some nearby observer. Nina's paranoia worked against her, the nerves making her already inexperienced hands shake, but she managed it.

The door opened with a soft click and Nina hurried inside.

As soon as she entered, she noticed the staleness in the air and the dust clearly visible as it floated across the rays of sunlight filtering through the windows. A coffee table in the living room—a battered old thing that looked just about ready to collapse—had a book on it. When she approached, Nina could see that the pages were yellowed with age and the spine of it was creased from use. There was a thin layer of dust on the cover, not quite thick enough to hide the title.

Something in Nina twinged in sympathy when she realized it was a photo album. With great care and a gloved hand, Nina opened the book and saw a picture of a smiling woman in a wedding gown. Fearnley stood by her side, arm wound around her waist and face looking brighter, younger—more alive.

Sarah, Nina remembered. His ex wife's name is Sarah. That was something that had only been mentioned once in all the articles Nina had read.

Fearnley must have taken one last look at the book—at all the memories he'd made and the life that had come crumbling down—before turning himself in. The thought made Nina's chest tighten and her previous beliefs on the type of man Fearnley was to solidify. For all that he had admitted to the crime, Fearnley seemed to have valued the simpler times. Enough so that tossing his connections aside seemed like a waste

Nina closed the book and walked away to inspect the rest of the place.

The kitchen was much the same as the living room. It was a small room, just large enough for a stove, a refrigerator, a bit of counter space, and a table just big enough for two. A single chair was neatly tucked in, seeming to wait for someone to occupy it. Nina wondered how long it would be until someone would do so.

Nina didn't find much in the kitchen, not that she expected to. She took only a minute to take in the small room before turning back to the doorway. Before she could walk out, however, something caught her eye.

Hanging on the wall between the counter and stove was a calendar. It was the type often given out by businesses at the start of the year, a different landscape for every month. November showed a lake surrounded by trees painted in warm tones that had Nina thinking of a forest in a painting. She shook the thought out of her head before it could lead her further away from the moment and instead walked over to the calendar.

There were a couple of days with Fearnley's messy scribble filling the small squares with everyday events. Nothing stood out to Nina as she read the cramped writing all about appointments and reminders Fearnley needed to keep track of—dentist's appointments, a meeting at work, someone's birthday—Katie, it said. Nina would need to figure out who that was.

His ex wife's name is Sarah, she reminded herself, and wondered if maybe he was seeing someone.

Nina found herself frowning as she reached up to turn the page back to the month of October. Again, there was not much that stood out when Nina went through the few reminders written there before turning back to September. Again, not much was found. Not until she got to the 20th.

Her eyes remained fixed on the date as some part of her mind helped her to connect the dots. After a second of simply standing there—time Nina didn't truly have—she pulled out her phone and opened up the notes she'd taken during her investigation of Alice had started.

"September 19th," she muttered to herself, realization dawning on her. Nina looked back up at the calendar. "September 20th, appointment at SEIN."

On that day, Fearnley had walked into the research center where Alice worked—had probably heard what happened to her and walked past a crime scene. Just one day earlier, he had killed Alice.

Nina let that thought sink in before walking back to the front door. She'd learned enough and had already been in the apartment for longer than she would have liked. Taking care to not be seen, Nina walked out. It was just a second after the door shut behind her that the one next door creaked open. The sound was enough to nearly make Nina jump, her phone close to slipping out of her hand. When Nina got a look at the woman who'd walked out she nearly laughed at herself.

She was a small woman with dark hair that was already streaked with silver. The woman was probably somewhere around sixty, if Nina had to guess, and had a lined, rounded face. When she spotted Nina, she seemed surprised. It occurred to Nina that she would of course stand out to someone who had lived in the building long enough.

"Oh, hello," the woman greeted. "Are you new here? I don't think I've seen you before."

Nina was smart enough to tell that the woman was vaguely suspicious. She didn't mind. It was, after all, a reasonable response. Especially given that the man who'd lived right next to her had been arrested for murder.

"No, I'm just visiting a friend," Nina said, doing her best to sound casual—to sound like she belonged. "Was just about to leave, actually."

The woman seemed to ease up just the slightest bit at that, and Nina wondered if she might be able to get something out of her. She lived next door from Fearnley, there was a good chance she knew something.

"Do you need help with that?" Nina asked, motioning to the large trash bag the woman had set down when she'd spotted Nina.

"Oh, no, it's fine. I wouldn't want to bother you," the woman said. She appeared more flustered, distracted from her previous suspicions.

"I don't mind. We're both heading out anyway," Nina insisted with the smile that usually served well to charm people. She reached over for the bag, the woman helping her pick it up. Nina waited for the woman to lock up and had her lead the way down the stairs.

She moved slowly, careful not to slip and gripping the handrail tightly. It reminded Nina of the overly cautious way her mother used to climb up and down the stairs of their home. Of the way Nina would hold her hand and her mother would smile down at her.

"I wish they'd fix the elevator already." The woman's voice snapped Nina back to the moment at hand. "Feels like it's been broken forever and all these stairs are hard on an old woman's knees," she went on with some humor lacing her complaints.

"Has it been out of order for long?" Nina asked, welcoming the chance to hold a conversation.

"'Bout a couple of months." They reached the second floor landing and Nina knew she had to hurry and get something about Fearnley before they stepped out of the building. "You'd think they'd get to fixing it by now, but then they hardly fix anything around here. But then the rent's so cheap. It's no wonder you get all sorts around here now a days."

"Is there a lot of crime around here?" Nina asked, curious. She knew the area had been a nice one before, but as with most cities, time had changed that.

"More than we used to get, though it's not so bad most of the time," the woman said. The first floor was within sight.

"My friend was just telling me someone from the building was arrested." Nina held her breath, waiting to see if the woman would revert to being suspicious, or if she would tell Nina what she needed.

"That'd be Mr. Fearnley." This time there was something in the woman's voice that told Nina she was familiar with the man, that maybe she knew something. "Just got arrested last month. Turned himself in, from what I hear."

"Fearnley? That name sounds familiar," Nina did her best to make it sound like she genuinely didn't know who Fearnley was. The doorway was just a few steps away.

"Oh, he's been all over the news. Killed that poor doctor, they say."

"I remember now. I haven't paid much attention to the news, but I remember hearing about that. Did he really?" Nina opened the door, the weak light filtering through grey clouds seemed blinding after spending so long inside the dimly lit building, and let the older woman walk out before her.

"Said he did. Honestly, it's hard to believe he would do something like that. Always seemed like a nice man."

"You knew him?" The woman smiled at Nina's question and stopped at the foot of the short series of steps outside.

"Lived next door to him for years. Sometimes he would help me fix things—little things—but it was more than what the landlord would bother with."

"He sounds nice," Nina's voice came out sounding just slightly softer than before, something she couldn't help as she remembered the man she'd talked to in prison and the book sitting on top of the coffee table inside of Fearnley's apartment.

"He was. Kept to himself most of the time, but I'd run into him all the time when he went to work. We'd chat sometimes, even after he came back from the hospital. Wasn't the same then, but he was still a nice man."

"What do you mean he wasn't the same." Nina cursed herself after asking that, thinking that perhaps she'd sounded a tad too desperate for an answer. The woman seemed not to have noticed. Maybe she just liked having someone to talk to.

"A lot of things happened to him, the kind of things that can change someone. Sometimes he looked sick to me, but I figured he was just on the mend after being in the hospital. He had an accident, you see. Still, hard to believe he could hurt anyone."

Nina knew what she meant. Maybe that was why she asked her next question.

"Do you believe he did it?"

The woman hesitated, her smile wavering and hands clutching her coat closer to her. Around them, the cold wind swirled, plucking the last remaining leaves from the tattered looking trees planted along the sidewalk.

"I don't know," she finally said, uncertain. She glanced back at the building they'd just exited before continuing. "To be honest, I don't think it was him."

Nina could hear her heart pounding in her ears and the world around her seemed to close off as the older woman in front of her became her only focus.

"Why do you say that?" Again, it took the woman a moment to gather her thoughts—or enough courage to speak.

"Well, you see, the walls are thin and because of the way the apartments are set up, I can always tell when he's leaving." She paused, looking sheepish at having admitted that she would—however unintentionally—pry into what her neighbors were doing. "That day they say he, well, you know, he got home from work same as always. I remember I was standing outside my door talking to Mrs. Gonzales from down the hall, and then he walked over—must have been getting back from work—soaked to the bone from the rain that day. We greeted each other like we always do and he went inside his apartment. Then, he didn't go back out again."

"And you're sure about that?"

The woman nodded. "I could hear the tv going next door. Didn't go to sleep until late because this knee of mine was hurting so bad and I know Mr. Fearnley didn't leave 'til the next day. Saw him leaving for work. Didn't look any different then."

For a second, Nina wasn't sure what to say to that. To hear that Fearnley could be innocent—that it was, in fact, a very real possibility—only raised more questions for Nina.

"You didn't tell anyone about that?" Nina asked, sounding more curious as to why that was than accusing.

"He confessed," the woman said with a shrug. "At the time I didn't think about it much. Probably because of the shock of it all. Now I think I should have said something." There was regret, deep and clear in the woman's eyes. Nina could understand, and at the same time wondered how someone could keep quiet.

Nina left the woman after that, with her thanking Nina for the help. She smiled, but Nina could see there was just the slightest bit of strain in it. There was guilt too, and Nina regretted having brought that feeling up.

Chapter 7

The headache Nina had been forced to endure for hours finally showed some signs of abating sometime soon. A likely cause of the pain, she knew, was thanks to the stress that the revelation of Fearnley's very likely innocence had brought her. Fearnley seemed to have something he wanted Nina to know.

Nina didn't remember much about the drive back home from Fearnley's apartment. It had all been a blur, her thoughts still swirling—unable to focus as the things she'd learned all clamored for her attention. By the time Nina had stepped into her apartment, her next task seemed clear and her mind felt just the slightest bit more settled.

She had to find proof that Fearnley was home when Alice was killed. Even if Fearnley's connection with Alice had nothing to do with the memories in Nina's mind, she knew the guilt of knowing Fearnley could be innocent would eat at her unless she did something. At that moment, Fearnley's face swam into her mind, his dull blue eyes still holding the look of defeat the man had worn when Nina had last seen him.

And then, Nina thought of the book on top of the coffee table in his empty apartment, gathering dust. Of the memories of his daughter Fearnley still held onto and the pain his family was most likely going through. Nina's resolve hardened at that alone.

Meticulously, Nina began organizing all of the notes and information she'd gathered on both Fearnley and Alice. Most of it were things released to the public in the various reports of Alice's murder. Then there was what Nina had found about Fearnley and Alice's past. All of that, she gathered with the knowledge that she'd need as many pieces as she could get to solve the puzzle.

Once that was done—and with the headache she'd been suffering from finally gone—Nina jotted down the timeline of events Fearnley's neighbor helped her uncover. Before she could do anything else, Nina knew she'd have to figure out just how much of what the older woman told her was true. For that, Nina would have to talk to Fearnley. Unfortunately, Nina didn't think she'd be able to arrange another visit, not when it had been hard enough to get the first one. She would have to wait—and hope—that Fearnley would want to talk to her enough to actually call her, as unlikely as that was.

Just as she was thinking this, Nina's cell phone rang. She nearly jumped, alarmed by the sudden sound, before picking up her phone—the caller was Nat.

"Hey, Nat," Nina said, doing her best to sound as normal as possible, despite her still rapidly beating heart.

"Hi, Nina," Nat sounded as she always did—happy, confident. Nina knew she should have felt happy to hear from her friend, but all she could think of were those mismatched eyes that seemed to stare right through her. She shook those thoughts out of her head to focus on the conversation at hand. "How have you been feeling?"

"Fine, I've been alright," Nina answered despite not feeling the least bit okay. "Haven't really done much, to be honest."

"Well, maybe that's for the best. You looked tired last time we talked."

"Yeah, sorry about that. It's just that a lot's happened and there's still a lot I have to sort out." Nina rubbed at her eyes, feeling the strain from all the hours of missed sleep.

"You mean like those dreams you were telling me about."

Nina froze for a second, the words sinking in slowly. She wasn't sure how to respond. A part of her wanted to reassure her friend, tell her she was fine for what seemed like the hundredth time—despite knowing she was far from it. Then, there was the other part of her that just wanted help. The part that needed someone to talk to, someone to listen to her and help her pick up the pieces.

But Nina knew she couldn't do that. Couldn't ask Nat to do that, of all people. She had enough to worry about in her own life.

"Yeah, well, at least that's settled now. They kind of went away on their own a while back. Must have been the stress." The lie came easily to Nina, something she was thankful for despite the slight twinge of guilt she felt at lying to her friend.

"That's good, though you should probably go back to get looked at by a doctor. Never hurts to be on the safe side," Nat said, and Nina smiled a bit at her friend's concern.

"Maybe later, there's something I'm working on right now that's keeping me busy," Nina said, with no intention of taking her friend's advice.

"Oh, have you gone back to work?"

For a second, Nina was about to tell Nat the truth. She'd taken more time off to recover, or so she'd told her boss. In truth, Nina just wanted more time. She needed to figure out what was going on with Fearnley and Alice and the mess inside her head before she was bogged down by more mundane stories at work. In the end, she found herself lying once more.

"Yeah, can't lay around the house all day for the rest of my life," Nina said. "Besides, I figured the stress of being cooped up in here all the time might have been making things worse." That much, at least was true.

"Guess that could be it. Are you working on anything interesting?"

Nina mulled over her answer for a bit before speaking. She decided it was as good a way as any to ask for Nat's opinion without making her friend ask any questions Nina wasn't ready to answer.

"I am. You might have heard about the case—it's been all over the news—about the doctor from the Institute of Neurology."

"The one who was murdered? I saw it the other day. They caught the killer already, didn't they?"

"He turned himself in." Nina found herself frowning at having to speak as if Fearnley was guilty when there was a good chance he wasn't. "His trial is set for later this month."

"Right, so you're reporting on the trial?"

"No, I'm actually looking into Fearnley, the suspected killer. Trying to find out what his motive was."

"They mentioned on the news the defence team would probably go for an insanity plea. Can't see how that would work, the guy looks sane enough and he's confessed," Nat said all too casually. It seemed callous to Nina, who had spoken to the man.

"That's just what the lawyers came up with, it doesn't mean it's true." Nina couldn't help but sigh a bit, frustrated just by thinking about it all.

"So you don't think their insanity plea will hold up?"

"Probably not." Nina had seen more convincing cases fall apart in court. Truthfully, Fearnley didn't stand a chance. Maybe that was why there was a sense of urgency following Nina as she worked through her investigation.

"Well then, good luck with your story," Nat said. She paused before continuing, "Just, don't push yourself too hard. You're still on the mend and honestly, this case sounds like a mess." Nina swallowed back a bitter laugh, thinking of just how well she knew that last part to be true.

"I've worked worse ones," Nina said with a small laugh that almost sounded bitter to her own ears. "I'll be fine. Besides, whatever the truth is, I'm sure it'll still make for a good story."

The call ended not long after, with Nina choosing to change the conversation to more mundane topics for a short while before Nat claimed she had to go. Nina was almost relieved to hang up. The effort of pretending to be fine was more exhausting than Nina could have ever anticipated. She wondered if Nat had noticed anything off with her, if maybe that was why she'd seemed to be in such a rush all of a sudden.

"Probably just busy," Nina muttered to herself. She rubbed the bridge of her nose, feeling what could only be the signs of an oncoming headache. Nina had to ask herself whether it was really the stress of everything bringing about the constant migraines.

With a sigh, Nina stood and headed to her medicine cabinet in search of something for her head. Over the counter pain medicine did little, but it was better than nothing. After that, she glanced at the time, noting just how late it was and for the first time realizing how hungry she felt. With no desire to prepare a meal, Nina decided to head out to a nearby shop.

The fresh air felt good as she stepped out, pausing for a moment to truly feel it sweeping over her. She breathed it in, catching the distinct scent that heralded oncoming rain. Thinking it best to make her improvised trip a quick one, Nina hurried on her way.

It was just a couple of blocks to the small fast food place Nina was heading to, the streets more crowded than usual as people got out of work and headed home or—like Nina was doing at the moment—stopped to pick up something to eat. No one paid any mind to Nina as she walked leisurely down the street until she reached her destination.

The place was small, with a brightly lit interior furnished with booths and a couple of small tables for two clearly visible through the windows lining the front. Nina had been going to the place for years, knew the old couple who owned the place, and could always trust in the food they sold to serve as a sort of pick me up whenever it was truly needed. She figured that was as good a time as any.

A bell atop the door jingled gently as Nina walked in and was greeted with the steady chatter of the people inside, occasionally punctuated by a laugh and accompanied by the steady clinking of utensils. The air inside was warm, carrying the scent of food and Nina felt comforted by the familiarity of it all. For a moment, Nina considered eating there, if only to prolong the small respite the place provided. In the end, she decided against that. After all, she still had work to do.

She ordered her food to go and sat in a corner booth to wait for her order to be ready. Her headache—she was happy to note—was all but gone, the constant throbbing in her head slowly dissipating until it was nothing more than a twinge that barely caught Nina's attention. Nina leaned back against her seat, closing her eyes for a moment as she basked in the brief period of near contentment she was in the midst of.

"Nina?"

Her hazel eyes opened at the sound of her name, the voice sounding familiar. Nina looked up with some surprise. Iris stood before her, coat pulled tight around her and a black and white scarf circling her neck, long dark hair spilling over it. Iris looked just as surprised to run into Nina there, but she was also unmistakably pleased. It was a feeling that Nina shared.

"Iris? Hi, wasn't expecting to see you here," Nina said, motioning for Iris to take a seat.

"Yeah, I didn't think we'd run into each other either, but I saw you through the window. Looked like you had something on your mind. How have you been?" Iris asked, smiling. She sat across from Nina, setting down a small bag from a bakery on top of the table.

"Fine, just came over to get some dinner."

"Didn't feel like cooking tonight?"

"I never do," Nina said with a wry smile. "What about you? I see you already have dessert." She looked pointedly at the bag Iris had walked in with.

"They're just some cookies my mom's been craving. I was thinking of visiting her today. I'd give you some, but you don't like sweets." Nina was amused to note that Iris seemed to be judging her for her taste.

"I like them in moderation," Nina corrected. Even she could hardly resist sweets every now and then, but she knew she didn't crave them nearly as much as her friend. It was a constant source of lighthearted arguing between her and Iris. "Are you ordering anything?"

"Oh, no. Not much point in it if my mom will just end up stuffing me with food when I visit," Iris said with a fond smile. "Just thought I'd stop by to say hi, since I saw you. You look good." Nina could tell Iris was taking the chance to look her over, her gaze lingering on Nina's eyes, below which she knew was the recent addition of dark circles. "Have you been getting enough rest?"

"A bit too much, to be honest." Nina wasn't lying. She napped a lot, found herself dozing on her couch more than she ever had, but the nights were too restless to get enough rest. That familiar hallway plagued both her dreams and her waking moments. Nina looked at Iris and found she didn't have the heart to tell her friend. "But I've been staying up lately. Figured I'd catch up on all the shows I've been missing while I'm still on leave."

"Just don't stay up too late," Iris said, looking the slightest bit more relaxed at Nina's excuse.

Before Nina could respond, her order was called, and she left Iris for a moment to pick up her food. When she turned back to her friend, Iris looked ready to leave. Nina met her by the door and they headed out together.

"Want me to drop you off?" Iris asked. "I parked just down the block."

"Thanks, but I'll walk. Some fresh air might do me good."

"Nina, we live in the city. There's no such thing as fresh air," Iris joked, lips curling into a smile.

"Still better than nothing." Nina shrugged, putting on a smile of her own. She waved to her friend as they parted ways and began her short walk home.

A part of Nina felt lighter after her run in with Iris. She felt like a piece of her old self had returned, the usual joking and casual chatting she did with Iris feeling natural. For a moment, she considered going back to work. Maybe having more mundane interactions—returning to her old routine—would help.

Then, she thought of Fearnley, and of Alice's face staring back at her through the mirror. Nina knew she couldn't just leave things as they were.

Night was rapidly settling around her, the sky darkening with every minute and the wind turning colder. Enough so that Nina was glad to reach her home. By the time she entered her apartment, night had fully arrived. The lights turned on automatically as soon as she opened the door.

The first thing Nina noticed when she walked in were the notes still spread out on her coffee table. She stared at the mess for a moment before moving on to the kitchen and choosing to eat there. As much as she wanted to figure out what was going on, Nina recognized that she needed to let her mind rest.

Already, Nina had allowed too much of her life to be enveloped in the mystery brought on by her—or rather, Alice's—memories. This thought was at the forefront of her mind when she passed the place where the picture of her and her mother had hung just days earlier. Now, there was just an empty space.

The rest of Nina's night passed without anything of note happening. Sleep didn't come quickly, perhaps because somewhere in the back of her mind, she was afraid of what she would see in her dreams. For once, though, there was nothing waiting for Nina on the other side of wakefulness. There was just an empty stretch of time, darkness, and then a sudden awakening—like blinking away the night.

Morning sunlight streamed through the window as the blinds opened and Nina became aware of the silence in her apartment only a moment before it was perturbed by the notice of an incoming call. On any other morning, Nina would have declined the call. That was not just any morning, and the caller was the one person Nina had been hoping to speak to.

Chapter 8

Fearnley sounded more tired than the last time Nina had spoken to him. The sheer exhaustion dripped from his voice as he gave an awkward greeting, as if Nina could ever possibly forget who he was. She could just about picture the thin man, fidgeting in his seat as he pressed the phone to his ear with a slightly shaking hand, shoulders hunched while the guard's stare pierced through him.

"I'm sorry to call you so early, Ms. Sheppard," Fearnley said, sounding uneasy. It was just past nine; Nina wouldn't have called it early. Still, she appreciated Fearnley's consideration.

"It's fine, Mr. Fearnley. I'm sure you didn't call without a reason." She waited for him to respond, deciding it would be best to let him lead the conversation. There was a notepad in her hand along with a pen. Nina was ready for whatever he had to say.

"No, I didn't," Fearnley paused. Nina wondered if he was just taking a break to compose his words. Perhaps the glare of the guard on his back made him uneasy. Nina couldn't blame him. "It's just,

I've been thinking, about our last conversation. About the memories I said were foggy."

Nina waited, trying to be patient when all she wanted to do was demand answers. She could hear Fearnley's breaths, could hear him swallow nervously and shift in his seat.

"Sometimes, I'm not sure about what I remember," Fearnley finally said. "I know I was there, I remember being there. I left work that day, and it was raining, they didn't say it would rain on the news, so I got soaked on the way there. And then I was talking to the doctor—I don't know about what, but she was upset—and then she looked scared, and I—" Fearnley cut himself off. They both knew what happened next.

"There was this loud bang," he went on after a moment's pause, voice sounding shakier than it had before, choked by the guilt he still carried.

"Then you left," Nina said, not wanting to make him relive the moment. "And you tossed the gun. They never found it, did they?"

"They didn't," Fearnley still sounded shaken. "But I don't remember the trip home all that well."

"Is that what you're not sure of?"

"No. That's not it." He let out a long breath after that, as if bracing himself for what he was about to admit. "Lately, I've had these memories—they come randomly—and I don't know what they are."

Nina held her breath, wondering if she'd been right. If maybe she wasn't the only one Alice had implanted memories into. She could feel her heart beating rapidly in her chest even as she did her best to remain calm.

"What do you see in them?" she couldn't help but ask, and was glad to note that her tone was far calmer than she felt at the moment.

"That day, I remember going home," Fearnley said. "I left work and it was raining, just like in my other memories. Only I didn't go to see the doctor, I went home. I know it sounds crazy, but I'm sure of it. I went home, and I didn't leave 'til the next day," he sounded just a bit desperate to have Nina believe him. Like he knew what he was saying wasn't possible, but was still certain it was the truth. "I swear I went home."

Nina felt her mouth go dry, her head spinning as she went over Fearnley's revelation. She heard him give a shuddering breath and wondered if the man was weeping. If the weight of it all was finally enough to make him crumble.

"I believe you," she said softly, meaning every word. "Mr. Fearnley, have you had any odd side effects since the surgery? Headaches, trouble sleeping, strange dreams?" He didn't respond for a minute, most likely thrown off by the question, but Nina had to know and time was running out.

"No, well, headaches I guess. Why does that matter? Do you think I'm going crazy?" Nina nearly laughed at that, a bitter laugh that would have been directed more at herself than at Fearnley.

"No, Mr. Fearnley, I don't. I just need to know if there are other instances of you having odd memories. When did you recall having gone home?"

"They—my memories about it from before—always felt wrong, and I'd get these headaches when I thought about that day. And then, a couple days ago things were clearer, only I didn't know what to do about it," Fearnley said after a moment of thought. "I still don't. I-I don't know why I called you."

"I'm glad you did," Nina said. "And this must all be confusing for you, but I promise, I will do everything I can to help. We'll get to the truth." Nina probably shouldn't have said that. A part of her screamed at her to stop, to not make any promises that she might not be able to keep. But she knew she had to give the man on the other end of the line something to hold onto. Some small hope to keep him from collapsing.

"It doesn't matter anymore," Fearnley said, voice sounding defeated—resigned to whatever fate awaited him. "Just, can you give my daughter a message? Tell her I'm sorry. It's her birthday next week." Fearnley's voice cracked, the pain in it raw. "I'm sorry."

Fearnley hung up, the click of it echoing around the room as Nina sat there, unmoving. She could still hear his voice, pained and much too brittle as he recounted what he'd done—or what he thought he'd done. It made Nina's chest tighten as a wave of sadness swept over her.

She sat there for a while longer, just until her overworked mind snapped back together. The things Fearnley had said—what he'd trusted Nina enough to confide to her—painted a clearer picture, even as she began to fear what the truth might really be.

Before she could really consider those things, there was something else that she needed to find out. After all, she had a message to pass along and no idea who Fearnley's daughter might be. Fearnley had hung up before Nina got a chance to ask, and none of the things she'd looked up about Fearnley had mentioned him having a daughter.

Maybe the girl lives with her mom, Nina thought, recalling Fearnley's estranged wife. She remembered the picture of a smiling woman in a wedding dress she'd seen in Fearnley's apartment, a wide smile that reached her eyes and made her look brighter spread across her face—tried to think of anything else she might have seen in that place that could hint at Fearnley's daughter.

And then, she remembered a calendar hanging on a kitchen wall. The small squares on it were filled with Fearnley's messy writing, reminders cramped together. Katie's Birthday, one of them had read, and Nina remembered wondering who Katie could be.

"It's her birthday next week," Fearnley had told Nina just minutes earlier, sounding absolutely shattered at the thought of not being with her on that day.

"His daughter's name is Katie," Nina said in a soft voice, the pieces coming together. Not wasting any more time, Nina began searching for the girl.

As it turned out, finding Katie Fearnley proved to be a far more difficult task than Nina first thought. There were no records of her as far as Nina could see. Not even an account on social media, much less an address. She would be, if Nina had to guess, starting college, judging by Fearnley's age and the amount of time since he'd married and divorced. Still, Nina could find no trace of her, no matter how much she scoured the lists of young graduates from local high schools, and later middle schools.

Maybe she took on her mother's name, she thought. It wasn't so uncommon, particularly at the time. More and more women had become reluctant to shed their name after marriage, some passing them on to their children. If Fearnley had divorced his wife, perhaps their daughter had taken her mother's name. Or maybe she did so after her father was jailed.

That was a possibility, the girl wanting to distance herself from her father in the wake of all the attention the case was garnering. Nina might have gone with that theory, but it just seemed wrong. Fearnley loved his daughter, Nina wanted to think she might love him just as much—that she wouldn't abandon him. Not to mention, that still wouldn't explain the lack of records on her.

I'll have to ask her mother, Nina thought. She'd been reluctant to speak to the woman, knowing from past experience that someone in her position wouldn't be so willing to talk to a reporter. There were already more than enough people trying to snag an interview with her, after all. Nina would have to think of a way to get the woman to listen to what she had to say and, hopefully, answer her questions.

Nina considered her options as she sat there, Fearnley's voice still ringing in her ears and the picture of a smiling bride flashing in her head. She briefly caught a slight hint of lavender in the air and wondered if she was going mad. The thought came easily enough that Nina was almost amused by it. With a sigh, she leaned back in her seat and closed her eyes, attempting to let them rest for a second, only to have Alice's piercing stare cross her thoughts. Her eyes opened in an instant and Nina knew couldn't afford to sit around and think for any longer. She needed a distraction.

Thankfully, delivering Fearnley's message provided the perfect one.

After not finding any other solution—at least, one that didn't require her to get any of her friends involved—Nina opted for the more straightforward approach. Even if she knew it would be a difficult one. The number she dialed was one she didn't know, one she'd had to dig up, and with each new number she entered, she wondered if anyone would even pick up the call. Each ring dragged on for much too long, and with every second that passed Nina considered hanging up. She considered letting the person on the other end of the line have just a bit more peace. Before she could hang up, the call was picked up.

"Hello?" The voice was hesitant, cautious. Nina knew there was reason for it to be so.

"Hello, Ms. Avila? I'm calling about your ex—"

"Are you a reporter?"

The question took Nina by surprise, though she should have expected something like that. Sarah Avila sounded cautious but, above all else, she sounded tired. Her soft voice was weighed down by the exhaustion that only someone going through an emotionally trying time could know.

"No, I'm not," Nina lied, convincing herself that she wasn't truly acting as a journalist at that particular moment. This had nothing to do with hunting down a story. It was all about connecting the threads to find the answer to what was in her head.

"Are you with the police then?"

"No, I'm just trying to pass on a message from Mr. Fearnley," Nina said before the other woman could cut her off. "You don't need to answer any questions if you don't want to. I'd just like for you to listen for a second. Please." She was still hoping Sarah would be more amenable to answering some things, but Nina wasn't holding her breath for that.

"What's the message?" Sarah asked after a moment. That note of caution she'd had from the start was still in her voice, but it seemed softer now.

"It's for your daughter, he wanted to apologize for missing her birthday." Nina felt more relieved than she would have thought at having successfully delivered the message, however indirectly. When Sarah didn't say anything for a while, Nina wondered if the idea of Fearnley keeping his daughter in his thoughts had truly affected her so much. "I'm sorry, this must be difficult for you," Nina started.

"No, it's not that," Sarah cut her off, sounding puzzled. "Are you sure that's what Chris' message? Did he say anything else?"

"He didn't, why?" Nina asked, her own sense of confusion rising. Sarah paused, hesitating. Nina heard her take a breath to compose herself.

"We don't have a daughter."

Chapter 9

Nina's head was spinning, the world falling away all around her as the words Fearnley's ex-wife had spoken echoed in her ears. Her stomach dropped, and a small twinge of pain shot through her head—along with the image of a small, pale hand reaching for a door knob and the messy scribble on a calendar that marked someone's birthday—before Sarah's voice brought her back to reality.

"We planned to have children later, once we felt we were more stable, but then we separated. Never had any children before that," Sarah explained. Nina only half listened, her mind still replaying the other woman's previous words.

"We don't have a daughter."

"Are you okay?" the question helped Nina ground herself. Her focus was back to the conversation she was having with Sarah.

"Yeah," Nina said, the word seeming distant even as she spoke it. Like it came from a mouth that was not her own—like a foreign face staring back through a mirror. Nina swallowed thickly, breathed out, and continued. "Yes, I'm fine. Did Fearnley know anyone named

Katie?" Nina asked, remembering the name written on the calendar in Fearnley's kitchen.

"Not as far as I know, but then I haven't really seen him in years. I only talked to him on the phone. Especially after the accident." She paused, Nina found herself holding her breath in anticipation of what the woman had to say. "I don't know who Katie is, but I can't imagine she'd be that close to him. His things are still in his apartment. I'm working on finding a place to store them. After he was arrested I was asked to look after his belongings. He didn't have anyone else he could ask." The words were spoken quietly, as if the very idea of what had become of the man she'd once loved hurt to think about.

"I'm sorry to hear that. What you're going through must be very difficult." Sarah let out a humorless laugh that rang with bitterness in Nina's ears.

"Yeah, you could say that." She sighed, a soft sound that was barely audible through the phone. "I don't know why Chris told you we had a daughter. Honestly, my guess is everything that's been going on is getting to him."

Nina didn't think that was the case. Something told her it wasn't as simple a thing as Fearnley slowly losing his mind. When she'd talked to him—his voice brittle and words grave—he'd sounded certain that what he was telling Nina was the truth, even if neither of them could truly understand what it all meant. So why then, would he mention a daughter he didn't have?

"Would you be willing to answer a couple of questions?" Nina asked, hoping Sarah would be amenable to that. The other woman took a moment to think about it and Nina was starting to brace herself for a refusal.

"Okay," she finally agreed. "What do you want to know?" Nina held back a relieved sigh and pulled the notebook on the coffee table closer.

"Did you hear from your ex husband at any time near the date of the incident?" She fidgeted with the pen in her hand as she waited for an answer.

Sarah let out a breath and took some time to think. Nina waited patiently, knowing she was fortunate enough to have the woman answer her questions.

"Yeah. Yeah, I did. He called about two days after . . . that. He sounded upset, said he'd been having odd dreams. Headaches too. I told him it was probably just some of the side effects from the surgery. That maybe the dreams were him remembering things. He trusted me enough to convince himself that was true. Guess I should have been the one to listen to him."

"You did all you could," Nina tried to comfort the woman. Even so, it was difficult to think of anything to say when her head was filled with thoughts of what could have possibly made Fearnley think he had a daughter when the only other person in his life was his ex wife. "Did he say anything after his treatment or have any other odd side effects?" She jotted down everything Sarah had told her so far, the scratching of her pen on the paper a sound that made it all seem just a bit more normal. Nina found she needed that small comfort.

"Ah, well, he had headaches, but that was pretty normal. I think he'd been warned about them from the start. I remember he mentioned trouble sleeping at some point, but he'd always had trouble with that some times, even before the accident. Might have been worse because of the dreams, now that I think about it."

"Did he ever tell you about the dreams he had?" For a second, Nina saw that hallway with the cream colored walls, the glimmer of a silver mirror just a few steps ahead and a green gaze. She closed her eyes for a second, and they were gone.

"No, he didn't go into any detail about those things. I think he wanted me to think things were fine with him, maybe he was afraid I'd stop calling if they weren't." Nina could hear what must have been regret at not having noticed that something was so very wrong with Fearnley after all. "Oh, wait, he might have mentioned something. It was before he turned himself in, and he didn't go into detail about anything. He just mentioned he'd dreamed of the place where he was being treated, but that was all. He didn't say anything else, and then he just sounded so upset I just changed the subject, tried to calm him down."

"He didn't mention anyone else? Did he ever talk about any of the doctors working with him?" What Nina truly wanted to ask was if Fearnley had mentioned Alice, but she thought Sarah might be wary of the name alone.

"He didn't talk about anyone unless I asked him if his doctors were treating him well. Never said anything bad about them either. Is there something I should know? About his doctors? Did they do anything to him?"

Yes, Nina wanted to say. But she knew she couldn't. Knew that having someone else poking around Fearnley's case wouldn't be helping her in any way. She knew that and yet the genuine concern in Sarah's voice nearly made her change her mind.

"No," she said instead, the lie flowing out of her mouth in a numb sort of way. "I'm just tryin to figure out what's going on. Thank you for talking to me, Ms. Avila."

"If you talk to Chris again," Sarah paused, seemed to think over what it was that she wanted to say, and then decided it wasn't worth it anymore. "Never mind," she said a second later.

Sarah hung up, and Nina thought she should count herself lucky to have even managed to speak to the woman for as long as she had. Nina stared at the notes she'd taken, attempting to think over the information she'd gathered while the same thought swam around in her head.

"We don't have a daughter."

Nina, closed her eyes, feeling a headache building up while a distantly familiar tune floated around her mind and crimson lips smiled at her. When her eyes opened, there was a feeling of unease settling in her chest. It was, she knew, the result of suddenly being so uncertain of what was going on.

She thought of Fearnley, sitting in prison while thinking of a daughter that didn't exist. Nina thought of the cruelty that would be telling him the truth—to tell him that all he had left was a lie. Nina found herself wondering what she would do if she were in Fearnley's place. Would she really want to know the truth then?

She thought of her father and the way they'd walk to the park when she was younger. His smile was wide when he looked down at her and his hands rough from his work, but warm—comforting—as they held her own much smaller hand. Then, she thought of her mother. Nina thought of watching her waste away as illness claimed her and how all that she'd had to comfort her were the memories of them talking in the kitchen while she watched her mother cook. The scent of spices coating the air and her mother's laughter like a melody in Nina's ears.

The memories made her eyes sting with tears that she fought to restrain as the fondness she held for those few fleeting moments—fragments of her life that made up the person that she had become—clashed with the thought of Fearnley sitting in his cell without knowing the cold reality that he would eventually have to face. For the first time in a long while, Nina questioned whether it wasn't better to live with a lie.

Green eyes flashed in her mind, boring into her. It was a gaze filled with a silent plea that Nina found difficult to refuse.

Whatever the answer that lay at the end of her search was, Nina knew she couldn't hide it. She couldn't ignore the fact that something was very wrong. She just had to figure out what that was.

"Pull the right thread and the whole thing will unravel," she re-membered one of her mentors telling her that years past. Nina would just have to stay true to that simple lesson and hope the thread she pulled next was the right one.

But how am I supposed to know? The thought stuck to Nina's already overflowing mind.

When it was all about her—about Alice and what seeing her face staring back at Nina meant—there was none of the pressure that she now felt mounted on her shoulders, none of the crushing knowledge that someone else depended on her.

Nina almost wished things were only that simple. A second after that thought crossed her mind, she almost felt like laughing. Things had hardly been anything resembling simplicity for a long time.

Not since before her mother had died, when the smallest od issues had seemed so much bigger in comparison to the relative peace that was her life. Almost subconsciously, Nina's gaze wandered over to the spot on the wall where the picture of her and her mother had hung not so long ago. The bare spot reminded her of Fearnley's appartment.

Despite being obviously lived in, the place had seemed barren—de-tached from anything that would have brought some warmth into the small space. There were no pictures on the wall, no hint of Fearnley ever having had anyone else in his life. Just a dusty album on his coffee table and the name of a daughter he never had scribbled lovingly on a calendar. The thought nearly made Nina want to cry.

It also brought up a thought that had been niggling at the back of her mind—a fear she'd pushed away until it was nothing but the barest of whispers amidst a howling storm of thoughts. Fearnley, timid but sane, had been so certain of the daughter he loved being real. Even so, the truth he knew was crumbling around him without him even noticing. How then, was Nina to know that the same didn't hold true for her?

I know who I am, Nina told herself, certain of her memories. But still that fear refused to disperse.

She ignored it for the time being, instead leaning back against her seat. Her eyes closed, an attempt to clear her head—something that became more and more difficult with every passing day. Against her will, her thoughts traveled to those she knew, those she was closest to. Her father's face, worn with age but still alive and bright eyed, smiled at her. The corners of his eyes creased and the laugh lines on his face spoke of a well lived life and of the things he'd overcome. She thought of her mother, back turned and the humming of a familiar song as she made one of Nina's favorite meals, calm as always. Stronger than Nina felt she could ever be.

Nina thought of Iris and the other people she worked with. People she saw every day and had gotten to know over the years. She thought of Nat, her childhood friend with whom she'd shared so much. The days they'd spent playing in a park and the mismatched eyes that seemed sharper than steel. And then, she thought of Ben, and found that she couldn't help but be glad he was still a part of her life despite the way things turned out between them. He was, after all, one of the connections that made her who she was.

"I know who I am," Nina told herself, this time out loud. The words rang loud with a conviction that had been absent from her since the day she'd awoken at the hospital—shattered and then clumsily put back together—with scars that ran deeper than anyone could know.

Nina knew who she was, knew who she had been before the world turned and knocked her off her feet. She just hoped that much remained true once all was said and done.

Chapter 10

Each step echoed more loudly than Nina would have thought possible. The sound seemed to bounce off the cream colored walls, amplified by the narrowness of the space she was in. It rang in Nina's ears, the sharp beat of it nearly drowning out the soft music playing from some as of yet unidentified source.

The notes drifted lazily, soft and tinged with a hint of melancholy that struck a chord in Nina. A faint sense of foreboding settled over her, distant enough that Nina paid it little heed. Her steps didn't falter for so much as a second, steady against the hardwood floor as they moved closer and closer to the end of the hall.

Three steps away.

Nina became aware of a scent in the air—of moss and earth and the smell of ozone during a storm. It was familiar, but still not something Nina could name the origins of. Like sand slipping through her fingers, the memory the scent might have invoked became but a passing thought.

Two steps away.

Nina could see the shining black frame hanging on the wall, the light glinting off the glass covering the picture inside. She felt a small twinge of what might have been relief and wondered where the feeling had come from.

And then, she was standing before the frame. The warm lighting of the hall washed over a painting of a simple landscape. A small cabin, a place that seemed to have stood there through many a summer storm and harsh winter snow, stood in the midst of trees colored in golds and reds with bark as dark as wet earth. The sky was but a sliver of blue-gray behind the warm tones overtaking the scene.

As Nina stared at the picture, a feeling of familiarity rose in her. Memories stirred in her mind, images she couldn't grasp. Her mind felt strange to her—unfamiliar. That sense of foreboding returned, clawing weakly at the walls of her mind, muffled cries of attention that Nina simply couldn't be bothered with. She stared at the painting, serene and composed, while feeling trapped for a reason she couldn't quite discern.

The painting faded, the music stopped. Nina opened her eyes.

She was still lying in bed, the room still dark around her with shadows seeming to dance as the lights from the street filtered through the small gap left in the middle of the curtains. Long silhouettes stretched up against the wall, like spectres watching Nina while she slept. A chill ran down her spine. Her heart pounded in her ears as, with shaking hands, Nina shoved the covers off and got out of bed.

The lights turned on once it was clear she was awake, just as they were programmed to do. The brightness was jarring, her eyes needing a moment to get used to the sudden change in lighting. She didn't bother lowering the brightness. It would help wake her up—keep her alert. Remind her what was and what wasn't, of where she was.

She made it to the bathroom even with her legs feeling unsteady and her heart still beating wildly in her chest. Immediately, Nina moved over to the sink to splash some water on her face. As the frigid water hit her skin, Nina couldn't help but wish that it would wash away those memories that haunted her still.

Water trickled down her face. Nina's gaze traveled up. Even as her eyes gazed into what was unmistakably her own face—hazel eyes ringed by dark circles in skin that seemed dull beneath the fluorescent lights—she felt a now well known fear creep into her. Green eyes flashed in her mind and it was all she could do not to scream.

She stared back at herself through the mirror, but all she could think about was Alice's unwavering gaze.

Nina felt her mouth open, a laugh pouring out of it all on it's own. It reminded her of how distant her actions had felt in her dream, like any semblance of control she'd ever had over her body was gone—disjointed emotions and actions that were not her own. The thought made her laugh turn into a desperate sound, broken and bitter. She briefly wondered if that was what it felt like to go mad.

She wondered if that was Alice's goal. If Nina would become a broken, nervous wreck like Fearnley once her mind could take no more.

I know who I am, Nina reminded herself. She didn't question the way that simple phrase had become so much like a mantra during the last couple of hours, echoing in her mind at the slightest sign that something was wrong.

After a couple of deep breaths, she was ready to move on with her day. There was too much left for her left to do. Things that mattered more than her own irrational fears.

The television turned on as Nina walked into the living room just a short while later. A cheery woman was talking about the newest celebrity gossip while her morning show co-host pretended to be interested.

"A source close to the couple claim the rumors are true. . ." the woman went on, sounding positively giddy. On any other given morning, Nina might have rolled her eyes and changed the channel. She didn't bother to do either on that day.

The curtains covering the large windows in the living room opened automatically to display the barely waking city stretching out for as far as Nina could see. In the distance, the first rays of the sun were just starting to emerge from behind the horizon, coloring the dark skyes with streaks of pink and orange. Nina might have thought it beautiful if her mind were not otherwise occupied at the time.

Nina forewent breakfast, even coffee seeming like too much of a bother, and instead headed straight to the notebook she'd left on the living room's coffee table the previous night. Her notes were still there, the same mess she'd walked away from with thoughts of the things written on those pages still filling her head.

The conversation she'd had with Fearnley's wife, Sarah, the previous day came back to her along with the harsh truth she'd discovered.

Still, sleep—however little Nina had managed to get—had done her some good. Nina knew he couldn't dwell on a single detail when there was still so much left to look into. So many questions that still needed to be answered.

"Pull the right thread," Nina muttered, even as she looked down at her notes with no idea on how to make sense of the information she'd gathered.

"...he was released on bail last night. His girlfriend of five years..." the woman on the television sounded downright giddy at the juicy bit of news. Nina was a bit amazed at how much someone could care about something so unimportant.

She sat on the couch after a moment, pulling the notebook closer, intent on writing down the latest of her dreams. Nina did her best to remember every detail. Every scent and sound and the feel of hair that was much too long to be her own as it slid over her shoulder. Every conflicting thought that appeared as she walked down that hall entirely against her will. She noted them all down despite the feeling of unease the very idea of them brought her.

It was just as she wrote the last of what she remembered and closed the notebook—the morning show ending and replaced by the news—that Nina received a message. The sound of her phone vibrating from atop its place on the table startled Nina enough to make her drop the pen she'd been using just a moment earlier. Once the beating of her heart had slowed and Nina had convinced herself that all was well, she picked up the slim device.

She'd received a message from Nat. It was short and simple, just as she'd expect of someone like her friend, who preferred to get to the point as soon as possible. As much as Nina couldn't help but smile a bit when she thought of her friend, she wasn't sure about accepting Nat's offer of lunch. There was a lot Nina still needed to do, a lot that she had to work out in her own mind. As much as she wanted to tell herself otherwise, Nina knew all too well that she wasn't in the right frame of mind to meet up with any of her friends or acquaintances. Not when her mind was still so badly fractured.

Not when she wasn't sure of who she could trust.

The most unfortunate part of that was that she really could have used Ben's help. If she wanted to know what Fearnley had been up to the night of Alice's murder, Ben would have been a great source of information. Still, Nina had not always had Ben around to help.

Just call him, some part of her mind whispered. Nina pushed the thought away, telling herself that she could do it on her own—that she'd done it in the past. That this time she had no choice.

Her gaze fell upon her phone, the temptation to ask for help calling to her. Iris was another good source. Nina was sure that her friend would be able to be of some help, but there was still that fear she'd pushed to the back. The one that screamed at her that it could all just be lie.

"We don't have a daughter." The words echoed in her head while an image of the broken man who lived a lie flashed before her eyes. Nina shut her eyes to try to get rid of it all and was rewarded with green eyes staring back at her. When she opened her eyes once more, she felt sick.

Nina sat there, trying to get a grip on her emotions—on her mind—and only ended up feeling drained.

". . .research shows. Further testing is being done. . . ." Nina was only faintly aware of the news anchor's voice, the sound distant as was the rest of the world as of late—muffled by the scent of spices and flowers and the sound of a piano that Nina couldn't see.

In a moment of clarity, she stood and walked out of the room. Nina soon found herself back in the bathroom, cold water running down her face for the second time that morning and her eyes refusing to look up at the mirror, afraid of what she—or rather, what her mind—would find there. Instead, she stared down at her hands as they held onto the edge of the sink, their grip hard against the cold ceramic.

It was then that Nina knew she couldn't stay there. She couldn't stay in that house, swarming with triggers to memories she didn't want to relive. She needed to get out, needed a reason to walk out. Nina thought of the things she'd learned, of the things she needed to know, and knew what her next move should be—she had people to call, an interview to arrange. But she wasn't going to do it there.

Without wasting more time, she got dressed, and gathered her phone and the notes she'd so painstakingly taken from the start of the whole ordeal. All the while, she didn't once stop to think about the bare walls that had once held snapshots of her most precious memories nor of the mirror not covered with a piece of cloth, all things she couldn't bear to see in her current state.

Nina didn't think about much but what she had to do as she shut the door of her apartment and continued on her search for the truth. A truth that some part of her feared would be far more cruel than she could ever expect.

Chapter 11

The light of the sun—for once not drowned out by ominous grey clouds—painted the world in overly bright colors that made Nina's eyes blur as a dull ache started up in her head. Nina simply pushed the pain away. She'd been doing that a lot as of late.

Still, she didn't pause to think about that. Nina didn't stop to think about anything but the task at hand, her steps never faltering for even a second as she made her way down the street. Her hand clutched the phone in her pocket and her eyes focused ahead as she walked past neatly trimmed lawns with scattered leaves painting them in golds and reds. She tried not to look at them, lest she be reminded of woods in the fall and a seemingly never ending hall.

The street was quiet, most people at work and school, and the only person she ran into as she walked from her car to the address on her phone was the mail carrier. Nina tried to act like the world wasn't crumbling around her as she pulled on a small smile and greeted the woman sorting out mail to be delivered. It was a simple action that took more effort than Nina cared to admit.

When she finally stood before the address she'd been looking for, Nina couldn't help but feel both relieved to be at her destination and anxious about what she would find there. She hardly wanted to consider what she would know by the time she walked back out of the white door of the modest—and completely unassuming—little home.

Nina walked up the short path to the front door, took a breath and let it out in one long exhale. Once she'd calmed herself, she knocked on the door, and waited. It was only a minute later that the door opened, and Nina found herself staring at a middle aged man with a tired look in his brown eyes. He was neatly dressed, though that didn't surprise NIna. who knew he'd been waiting for her. She still appreciated the effort.

"Good morning, Mr. Sadeghi. I'm Nina Sheppard, we spoke over the phone." Nina wondered if he would ask for her credentials. She was prepared to show them, of course. She just hoped he wouldn't call her workplace only to find out she was on leave.

"Yes, I've been waiting for you. Come in, please," the man said, stepping aside to let Nina in.

She stepped inside and immediately felt the warmth of the home wrap around her—a comforting sensation she needed more than she would have thought.

"I hope I'm not bothering you," she said as she removed her coat, mostly out of politeness than because she truly cared.

"No, it's fine. I've been taking some time off from work to deal with ... things." He led her away from the entrance and into a small but comfortable living room. The scent of freshly brewed coffee hung in the air, enticing and calming to Nina. "Please, have a seat."

Nina sat on a couch that felt far more comfortable than her own. She supposed it was probably because of the long hours she spent on it pouring over information on Alice and Fearnley.

"Would you like a drink? Tea, coffee?"

"Coffee would be great, thank you," Nina said, hoping the drink would help her feel more at ease.

Sadeghi left the room and Nina was left to sit and take in the room she was in. The place made her think of Fearnley's apartment, though it wasn't so much because of the similarities as it was because of the differences between the two. The room she was sitting in felt arm, lived in, memories of the people who lived there woven into every inch of it. From the corner of her eye, she could see what were undoubtedly pictures hanging from the wall—pictures she didn't have the courage to look at directly. Once again, Nina found herself thinking of the bare walls in her home for a moment before she was back in the hall, steps echoing and the glint of silver just ahead.

"Here you go."

Nina nearly jumped at the sound of Mr. Sadeghi's voice, too caught up in her thoughts to have heard him return. She blinked away the distant look that had been in her eyes and watched as a tray with two cups of coffee was set before her on the coffee table.

"Thank you," she said, taking her cup and not bothering to add anything to it before taking a small sip. Nina could feel the hot drink running down her throat, warming her from the inside. When she set down the cup, she found she felt a little more like herself.

Across from her, Sadeghi took a seat in a worn looking armchair. His movements were slow, like the simple action expended too much effort. He let out the slightest of sighs and didn't bother with the coffee in front of him.

"You said you wanted to talk to me about Chris," he said, looking wary of what would come next. There was still a determined look in his eyes, one Nina saw as a hint of what the man was truly like, shining through the worn exterior.

"Yes. Would you mind if I record the conversation? It's to ensure accuracy and context," she clarified, pulling out her phone. Sadeghi hesitated for a moment before agreeing. Nina set her phone to record and placed it on the coffee table. "As I understand it, you worked with Christopher Fearnley for some time."

"I did," was the man's simple response. He paused, looked down at the cup of coffee he'd left untouched and then focused his gaze back onto Nina. "I don't really know what I can tell you about it. The cops, the reporters, they asked about him when this all started. They asked most of the people who knew him."

Nina was aware of that. That was, after all, how she'd come across Sadeghi's name. Back when the whole mess had just started—when piercing green eyes had yet to burn themselves into Nina's mind—Nina had read an article about Fearnley and his supposed crime. Sadeghi had been interviewed briefly, had sounded like he knew Fearnley well enough.

Maybe it was a desperate move on Nina's part. Maybe she was wrong and the two men had barely spoken to each other. Either way, she figured it wouldn't hurt to ask a couple of questions. Even if the only reason she'd thought to do so was to get out of her own apartment.

"Did you speak to him often?" Nina asked.

"Yeah, we worked together so we talked all the time. He didn't mention anything odd, if that's what you're thinking. I had no idea of what he was going to do." Sadeghi looked truly distressed by the idea. Nina, of course, believed him. There was nothing for Fearnley to say about a crime he most likely didn't commit.

"I'm sure you wouldn't know anything about that," Nina tried to reassure the man. "I just wanted to ask you a bit about his daily habits. How he was at work, the people he knew, that kind of thing. We're doing a profile on him, trying to get a different perspective. Nothing you need to worry over." Nina thought her cover sounded likely enough. It certainly sounded like something she would be tasked with covering.

Sadeghi seemed to calm a bit at that information, the grip he'd had on the couch's arm rest loosening the slightest bit and the look in his eyes losing a bit of it's edge. He let out a breath and gave a small nod, one Nina almost missed.

"Right, well, I suppose I would know a bit about that. I, um, I'm not sure how much detail I can go into."

"Anything you can tell me is fine," Nina said. "What would you say he was like? Was he a good man, friendly? Did he keep to himself?"

"He kept to himself for the most part, but he was nice enough once you got to know him. Chris was a private person, didn't talk much about his private life but he did tell me about his divorce. That was about all most people knew as far as his home life went." Nina nodded, noting how Sadeghi seemed more at ease as he spoke.

"What about after the accident and surgery? Did he seem different to you?"

Sadeghi paused to think about it while Nina waited patiently. She sipped from her cup of coffee, savoring the earthy taste of the brew while she waited for an answer.

"I guess he was quieter. But, it seemed like he had a lot more to think about so no one really blamed him for it. He still worked hard, did what he had to. Other than that, there wasn't much change."

That fit into what Fearnley's neighbor had said. There had been a change in Fearnley, small but still there. Nina supposed that was true enough for her as well.

"Did he ever talk about the accident or his recovery?"

"No, I don't think it was something he wanted to talk about. We didn't ask. Most people didn't know him well enough to anyway."

"Did he mention any headaches, trouble sleeping, other strange side effects?"

"He'd get migraines sometimes, yes. I asked him about it once and he said it was a side effect, that the doctors told him they'd go away in time. Never mentioned any trouble sleeping, but now that I think about it he did look tired when he returned to work. I just thought it was the strain of everything that happened. Could have been from insomnia."

Or dreams that aren't dreams after all, Nina thought. She shoved the thought away, not wanting to be bogged down by her own problems.

"Did he mention any new acquaintances? Maybe someone named Katie?"

Sadeghi looked confused by the question. He still thought about it before giving his answer, something Nina appreciated.

"No, at least, I don't remember him saying anything about meeting anyone." Nina nodded, not surprised by the answer in the least.

"What about his work? Did you notice any change in the way he worked or was he the same?"

"I'd say it was the same. He was very focused. Maybe working kept his mind off things." Nina had no doubt that it did.

"On the night of the incident, did you notice anything off about him? Any changes in his attitude or schedule?" Nina already suspected what the answer would be. She still couldn't help but feel just the slightest bit of anxiety as she waited for the man to speak.

"No, he left at the usual time. He was always careful to leave early enough to catch the bus. That night was the same."

"He didn't drive to work?" Sadeghi shook his head.

"His car broke down last year and he didn't bother getting a new one. A couple of people offered to drive him home after he returned to work, but he always said he didn't want to be a bother." Nina saved that information for later, an idea already occurring to her.

"I think that's enough for today, Mr. Sadeghi. Thank you for speaking to me," Nina said, picking her phone up from the table at the same time that she set down her nearly empty cup of coffee. She heard the man sitting across from her release a relieved sigh.

"I'm sorry I couldn't go into much detail," he said, standing from his seat as Nina did the same.

"No, there's no need to apologize. You were a great help." Nina walked with him to the door, taking her coat and pulling it on while Sadeghi stood there, seemingly lost in thought. Nina found herself wondering what kind of thoughts the faux interview might have brought up for the man.

Maybe he thinks he didn't know anything about Fearnley after all, she thought.

Whatever the case might have been, he didn't say anything else about Fearnley, and Nina soon found herself standing outside. The day was still much too bright for her, but she felt more at ease. Perhaps it was because of a renewed sense of purpose that came from knowing what to do next.

"Again, thank you for your time, Mr. Sadeghi." She stood before him as he held the door opened, looking just as tired as when she'd first arrived at his doorstep.

"It's no problem, Ms. Sheppard. Thank you for listening to me. I think I needed to talk to someone—anyone—about what happened." His grip on the door tightened, his lips forming a tense line. "I don't think I knew Christopher all that well, but he wasn't a bad man. At least, I didn't think he was. It's been confusing, everything that's happened."

Nina nodded, knowing full well how difficult it could be to reconcile something like what Fearnley was accused of, with any preconceived ideas of that person. Sadeghi would always think about what Fearnley had done, what hints there could have been. What he might have been able to do to stop Fearnley, if only he'd paid more attention. She almost wished she could tell him what she knew.

Instead, she bid him goodbye and walked away.

The door closed shut behind her, a soft sound that almost echoed in Nina's ears. She was back out in a too bright world she no longer felt she belonged in. Nina stuck her hands into her coat's pockets and walked down the walkway of Sadeghi's house and into the sidewalk. The streets were as desolate as when she'd first arrived, and Nina found herself feeling grateful for the bit of solitude.

As she walked away from the house, her gaze focused away from the fall colors around her, her mind mulling over what her next step would be.

Chapter 12

The man on the other side of the counter stared at the picture on Nina's phone while a young girl walked by behind him, boxes in her arms and a curious look in her brown eyes. The man's dark eyes swept over every feature of the man on the image, taking it in and running the face through his mind. Nina stood by, patiently waiting and watching for any reaction that might surface on his face.

"Yeah, he came by here," the man finally said. He handed Nina back her phone with a hand roughened by years of work. "He was standing outside, waiting for the bus. It was really coming down that night so I didn't mind him hiding from the rain up in the front. Didn't say anything though, just stood there until the bus came."

"Do you remember the approximate time he spent standing out-side?" Nina asked, only to receive a shrug from the stout man.

"Couldn't say, just remember it was sometime past six." He raised a hand to scratch at his stubbled chin, a thoughtful look on his face.

"It was nearly seven."

Both Nina and the man she'd been talking to looked over to the young woman who'd spoken, the same one who'd walked past just a minute earlier. If the faded red apron she wore was anything to go by, she also worked at the mini market Fearnley had stood outside of. Though she'd peered at Fearnley's picture when Nina had shown it to the other man, but hadn't said anything at first.

"The news was ending and they were about to play that one show with the vampires. The one you always make fun of," she went on once she'd gotten their attention. She pointed up at the dusty television set up on one corner behind the counter. On the screen, an advertisement showed a woman driving past the woods. The image of trees covered in leaves of red and gold flashed briefly through Nina's mind.

The thought was gone in an instant, like a phantom pain one couldn't be sure was even there. Nina shook it off, focused on the moment.

"Oh yeah," the man agreed after a moment of thought, seemingly failing to notice Nina's momentary lapse in attention. Nina jotted down the time she was given and turned to the young girl.

"Did you talk to him, by any chance?" She received a nod from the girl.

"Asked him if he wanted to come in while he waited for the bus. It was freezing that night. He thanked me, then said he didn't want to be a bother, and then I had to get back to work. A while later I looked back and he was gone."

"Did either of you see him leave?" They shook their heads.

"The bus is usually on time. Should have been here 'round seven," the man said. Nina nodded, made a note of the time the bus usually arrived and looked back up at the two employees.

Curiosity was splayed across their faces, questions about Nina's purpose just barely held back. She thanked them and left the small shop before those questions could be spoken. Nina could feel the two employees watching her as she walked back out into the cold, bustling streets.

The place where Fearnley normally waited for the bus was on a fairly busy street, shops lining the sidewalk. Nina could just picture the way their neon signs would have lit the street on the night Fearnley stood in front of that mini market—waiting in the rain and wanting for nothing else but to go home. She glanced up, the awning of the thrift store she was standing in front of helping to camouflage a camera. Not for the first time, Nina wished she could have access to the area's CCTV footage.

Not for the first time, Nina wished she had Ben or Iris' help.

She wasn't going to dwell on that though—or on why she couldn't depend on them. Not then. Instead, she went back to her car and drove off to where she knew Fearnley would have gotten off the bus on the night Alice was killed.

The drive was short thanks to the lack of traffic at the time. Fearnley didn't live too far from where he worked, just far enough that most people wouldn't bother walking instead of taking the bus. As Nina walked from her car to the bus stop, she took in her surroundings.

A two story apartment building painted in peeling, off white paint stood on the corner where the bus stop was placed. Most of the street was lined with apartment buildings, houses, and a small shop or two. It was a relatively peaceful place, with only the usual sounds of the street as cars and buses drove by and the distant sound of a police siren. Nina could see only a couple of people walking by—a woman with grocery bags in her hands, children riding their bikes after leaving the corner store.

For a moment, Nina was reminded of the place where she grew up. She was reminded of a street much like the one she was standing on, the sounds and sights much the same though seen through a young girl's eyes. She could almost hear her mother humming in the background and then there were green eyes staring at her and Nina was thrown back into a hallway that she didn't want to walk down anymore.

She blinked and it was all gone, even as the beating of her heart seemed wild in her chest. Nina felt a shiver run down her spine and struggled to focus on the world in front of her—on what was real. Then, the moment was gone, and she was left feeling empty and exhausted as those intrusive thoughts and memories faded without a hint of ever having been there in the first place.

Nina took a moment to fully calm herself before she continued on her way.

Her steps were shaky at first, the weight of what she'd just experienced still sitting heavily on her shoulders. But Nina shook it off and concentrated on the moment. She concentrated on the thrift store across the street from the bus stop.

The place was small and crowded, with all sorts of items placed without any clear sense of order and a rack full of Halloween costumes by the front of the store. Amidst the cluttered mess, a woman walked out. She was an older woman, dark hair tied back, strands of it falling into her rounded face.

"Hello, how can I help you?" the woman greeted, her accent thick and her smile welcoming.

"Hello, I was hoping you could help me out with a bit of information," Nina said, pulling out her phone. "Have you ever seen this man?" Nina held out her phone, Fearnley's photo brightly displayed on it.

The woman took it and had only to glance at it for a second before Nina saw recognition sweep over her face.

"Yes, I know this man. He comes here sometimes, but I haven't seen him in a while." Nina supposed it made sense for Fearnley to frequent the place when he lived so close to the shop.

"Do you remember when you last saw him?" Nina asked. The woman's eyes narrowed, her mouth twisting just the slightest bit as she studied Nina.

"Why? Did he do something?" the woman answered Nina's question with one of her own.

"He's been accused of murder," Nina answered, the words sounding wrong to her own ears. The woman's face changed in an instant, her brow rising and eyes widening, lips parting just the slightest bit as a breath left her. "I'm writing an article on him and trying to piece together where he was on the night of the crime. Did he pass by here around a month ago?"

The woman seemed to think about it, her mouth twisting into a frown while her eyes fixated on the picture staring back at her from the phone's screen.

"He came here a couple times last month, but I wouldn't know when. Maybe at the start of the month. I only remember he bought a coffee maker around the first week of September. We had a new shipment," she finished with a shrug.

Nina couldn't help but feel disappointed—she suspected she even failed to hide it at all—but she knew she wasn't at a dead end. There were still other places nearby where Fearnley could have stopped by on that rainy night.

With a sense of resignation settling over her, Nina began to turn, intending to head back out and already thinking of where she would go next. Her gaze traveled over the items in the shop, racks of clothing, stacks of board games, shelves filled with household items. Then, her eyes fixed on something—a single, narrow shelf in the corner by the door. It was filled to the brim with books of all sizes, dusty from sitting there for so long.

A single book instantly grabbed her attention, the word she'd been mulling over what felt like forever sticking out in bold yellow letters on a pitch black cover. Almost all on their own, her feet led her closer to the case, her hand rising to grip the spine, dragging out the book and leaving a streak through the dust that had settled on the case.

The Mechanics of Memory, the cover read, the silhouette of a person and a stylized image of the brain on it. The book was worn, as were most things in the shop, used but still well cared for. The spine was hardly damaged and the greatest hint as to it having been used before was the very tip of a single corner being folded so badly it was close to falling off. Nina didn't mind it, didn't care about the insignificant amount of damage nor the dust still clinging to it.

"How much for this book?" she asked, turning back to the shop owner.

A moment later, Nina walked out of the shop with the book clutched in her hand. She hadn't found out anything of value really, at least, not from the woman at the thrift shop. Still, she had the knowledge that Fearnley had gone home on that night when everything had gone wrong. Nina had the testimony from Fearnley's neighbor that he had, in fact, arrived home at the usual time. With the timeline she'd managed to make, Nina could be sure that Fearnley couldn't have gone to see Alice at any point before she was found dead.

With that knowledge, and a new bout of exhaustion sweeping over Nina, she made her way to her car instead of continuing to wander around, asking about a man she hardly knew. The sun was just setting, painting the sky in all shades of pink, and red, and orange. Nina would have thought it beautiful if not for the flash of a forest in warm tones that the sight invoked.

She climbed into her car, her head twinging in pain and the book still clutched in her hand. Nina leaned back against her seat, breathed out, and glanced down at her recent purchase. After staring for a moment, she lifted it and flipped it open to the index. Various topics on the workings on the mind and the nature of memories met her gaze.

"Synapses, episodic memory," Nina read out a couple of the chapters. "Reinforcing memories, memory triggers." Nina paused. She looked at the page number and searched for the chapter, finding it only a second later. After skimming the first page, Nina folded a corner of the page and closed the book, tossing it onto the empty seat next to her.

As the sun sank behind the horizon, it's last rays of light glinting off the glass of the shop windows around her, Nina drove off, intent on heading home. She had some reading to do and a new hope that maybe she could get some answers.

Chapter 13

"Research points to it being a viable treatment for those suffering from trauma. . ." the woman on the television screen read the words with a false interest that Nina had grown all too accustomed to hearing. The background noise still helped her remain calm. Helped her not to feel so alone in the world as she sat on her couch with a second hand book in her hand. It's yellowing pages, she hoped, could hold some piece she was missing of the puzzle that Alice had left behind.

Smell, sights and sounds may all act as triggers for memories. Sensory information—particularly olfactory—has been proven to create more vivid memories while also increasing the speed in which these memories are recalled.

Nina's mind tried to process the information through the fog of exhaustion and confusion that had refused to dissolve for the last couple of days. A yawn escaped her mouth, and not for the first time, she considered heading to bed. The reminder of what would most likely occupy the place of her normal dreams was enough to make her turn back to her book and keep reading, even as her eyes burned and she struggled to keep them open.

"The next commissioner of the FDA is rumored to be. . . ."

The words seemed to blend together as Nina's mind disengaged with what she was reading. Her grip on the book slackened, fingers relaxing and the text slipping past them to fall onto the rug beneath Nina's feet with a muted sound. It was enough to rouse Nina from the dazed state she was in. She jerked into a more upright position, her eyes opening fully. For a moment after being startled, she was alert, uncertain of her surroundings.

For the second time, she was startled as the coffeemaker let out a beeping sound, alerting her to a new pot of coffee being done. The scent would have been enough to tell her as much. It was rich and earthy and something Nina sorely needed at that moment.

Nina got up, picked up the book she'd let slip, and walked off to get some coffee, hoping it would keep her awake for a while longer. Her movements felt odd, distant, almost as if she were not fully in control of her own body. Her mind—so completely filled with thoughts of Alice and Fearnley, and the doubts and fears that kept building up inside of her, so close to overflowing—seemed to be in a place separate from the rest of her. Not for the first time, Nina couldn't help but feel like a fragment of who she had once been.

Perhaps the thought might have hurt more before everything in her life had changed so drastically. Before she'd gotten so used to being unable to recognize herself.

The drink was too hot still, but Nina felt refreshed from the first sip of the bitter liquid. It slid down her throat and warmed her, made her feel awake—alive. The small tremors in her hand, something Nina had gotten used to after it had persisted for long enough, seemed to calm just the slightest bit.

"Tell us about the film," came the voice of an over enthusiastic woman from the television. Nina could just about hear the wide smile on her face. Red lips flashed in her mind, a smile that seemed a bit too wide, eyes that pierced through her.

She faltered, swaying on her feet. The coffee she held splashed over the rim of the cup, scalding the skin of her hand. Nina kept her grip on the cup, somehow managed to stay on her feet, and then the world righted itself and her mind was her own, though a dull ache had begun to build up in her head.

"What makes the character you play so special?" the woman was asking now. Nina made a conscious effort not to listen too closely. Not to think about the fake smile that would be plastered on her face still.

Nina set the cup down, her skin still much too hot and the pain just registering in her mind. A familiar heat that threatened to send her mind reeling into yet another memory she would rather not recall. Already she could recall the acrid smell of the smoke—taste it in her mouth as a cry for help was muffled. She stuck her hand under the tap, water flowing out of the it and splashing onto her skin before it hit the sink and swirled down the drain. The cooling sensation of the water on her skin was enough to snap Nina out of the moment she'd momentarily found herself stuck in. A moment she wished had been one of the many wiped from her mind.

"It's a complex role, I can't say it hasn't been a challenge to get into the character's head. . . ." The woman, a young actress with a voice clear and delicate, like bells, laughed. "She's in her head a lot, so it's hard to know what her true motives are."

Nina fully emerged from the kitchen, her hand feeling better though a dull burning sensation persisted. Her mouth tasted like coffee—bitter—and yet felt too dry. Nina focused her gaze on anything but the television, walked to the couch and picked up the book once more before changing the channel.

". . .In that way the narrator is not a reliable source. . ." said the man on the television, an older gentleman with a stern look on his aging face. It was the kind of person Nina fully expected to see on a channel that specialized in educational programming. Still, his steady voice was pleasant enough that she didn't bother to look for something else.

Instead, she looked down at the book in her hand, her thoughts clearer for the time being. She thought of the smell of flowers and spice and the soft piano notes drifting down a narrow hall. Nina thought of the clacking of her shoes on the hardwood floors and of Alice who would know all too well what the book Nina held was talking about.

Alice, who had left Nina with a series of vivid memories for a reason Nina still wasn't certain of.

The scent of coffee still permeated the room. Coupled with the steady, soothing voice of the man on the television, Nina felt herself getting drowsy. She could feel the warmth of her apartment wrapping around her like an embrace, thet sounds of the city were just barely audible, seeming much more distant than they really were. Nina closed her eyes and pictured the moment as it was, painted vividly in her mind by the scents and sounds that surrounded her. Each sensation adding a stroke of color that made the picture all the more clear.

Her mind switched for the briefest of moments to the picture of the woods hanging in the hall of Alice's memories, and in that instant, Nina caught a glimpse of what Alice might have been thinking.

She wanted the memories to be clearer, Nina thought, her eyes opening and staring at the television screen without truly seeing the images on it. Her mind was somewhere else, her thoughts focused on the stray thought.

She wanted me to remember. To have to see those memories over and over. The thought was one that almost made Nina upset. Alice's memories had been meant to haunt her, to become so ingrained in her thoughts that Nina wouldn't be able to escape them—that they would drive her mad. And maybe they drove Fearnley mad.

The thought made a shiver run down her spine, the warm room suddenly seeming much too cold and the sound of Fearnley's voice—of a man on the verge of breaking apart—seemed to ring in Nina's head.

But I still don't know if Alice really implanted the same memories into Fearnley. What if it's something else? What if we're both just going mad? The thought was of little comfort to Nina. Especially because there was too much evidence pointing to something else—something bigger than her and Fearney and Alice, going on. Even so, she knew it wasn't enough. Nina knew there was more left to uncover before she could get the bottom of it all.

She just hoped she could keep herself together for long enough.

"...The journey home is a long, yearly ritual. ..." Nina turned off the television, the voice of a woman on some sort of nature show cutting of abruptly. The sudden silence seemed almost oppressive, reminding Nina of just how alone she was.

It's never bothered me before, she told herself. Just another thing that had changed as of late. Something Nina wished could have remained as it once was.

She glanced at the cellphone laying on the coffee table, still and silent as the rest of Nina's home. For an instant, Nina thought about calling someone, anyone. Maybe Iris, her cheerful demeanor would help and Nina could bounce ideas off of her. Or Ben, who Nina was sure she could convince to get her some information, despite all the complaining he would inevitably do. Her fingers twitched at the idea, eager to dial a familiar number. Instead, she closed her eyes and felt glad she'd powered down her phone earlier.

Nina walked away, knowing it was too late for any calls. That it was too risky to involve anyone else. She glanced at the clock on the wall, the late hour finally convincing her to finally get to bed. With some reluctance, Nina made her way to bed, doing her best not to think about where her dreams would take her.

She set an alarm for an hour that was too early for someone as tired as her to wake up. Still, Nina didn't want to dwell on unpleasant dreams—or memories. As soon as Nina closed her eyes, sleep took her.

The hall was the same as it always was, the lighting warm and the cream walls spotless. Ahead, Nina could see a picture frame hanging from the wall, still too far for her to be able to tell what it was that the frame held. A welcoming scent drifted in the air, a delicate aroma of spring flowers that made Nina's mouth curve into a small smile. Faintly, she could feel some emotion, pleasant yet distant. Like a memory she couldn't quite grasp before it slipped from her fingers like sand. Some happy moment that was on the verge of being forgotten. It was there for a second, and then Nina was making her way down the hall, her steps quick and the clacking of her shoes on the hardwood floor bouncing off the walls.

She walked down the hall with a purpose, steps never faltering and eyes focused on the door at the end. A door that Nina had hardly ever paid any attention to, always focused on the frame hanging on the wall. On the scents and sounds that stirred feeling foreign to her. On the diluted fear that gripped her the moment she found herself in that hall, like a passing thought that was absent for once.

A foreign sense of anticipation built up inside of her, Nina's heart beating in her chest. Hair brushed against her cheek and Nina felt a laugh was bubbling up inside of her, bursting out in a childish giggle that sounded like chimes caught in a summer breeze. The scent of spring flowers was all around and Nina felt at ease as she rushed past the frame hanging on the wall.

The door was in front of her, close enough to touch. Nina reached out with a small, pale hand, the doorknob cool as her fingers slipped around it. There was a creaking sound, the doorknob turned, and then there was light spilling from the opening—blinding in its intensity. Anticipation, pure and unrestrained, filled her for a second before it all faded away.

Nina awoke before the alarm she'd set had even gone off, the blinds covering the city were still shut. Her heart was beating in her chest, though not nearly as quickly as in other occasions, the familiar sense of panic that accompanied Alice's memories absent—a rare occurrence. Still, Nina found her mind going over the dream once more. She held out her hand—dark skinned, with faint scars she did her best to cover—so different from the one that had opened the door in her dream.

The scent of spring flowers was still clear in her memory, so vivid she could almost smell it as the giggling of a child rang in her ears. Vivid fragments of a life that was not her own. Nina sat in her bed while the sun rose over the horizon, painting the city in warm tones of orange and gold. The city was waking, and with it Nina was just starting to understand.

Chapter 14

There were two missed calls and a couple of messages on Nina's phone when she woke up and decided to turn it on. She still felt sluggish, the coffee she was in the process of drinking just starting to kick in and it was too early to check all of the calls and messages from her friends that she had missed while the device was powered down. Nina didn't want to deal with the guilt that came from cutting herself off from them.

She felt grateful that they hadn't decided to show up on her doorstep yet, but she supposed it was still too soon to feel relieved about that. A small quirk of her lips was the only hint of Nina's amused fondness toward her friends. That very fondness was one of the reasons why she was so glad to have decided not to involve them in the mess she was currently caught in.

"Research is still being conducted at the South East Institute of Neurology. . ." said the woman on the television, dark eyes staring straight ahead as she sat behind a gleaming desk, most likely reading off of a teleprompter. Despite knowing the woman's gaze wasn't fixed on her, Nina still found her stare unsettling. At the mention of the same place where both her and Fearnley had been treated—the place where Alice had worked and died—Nina ignored that and instead stared at the screen.

"Testing is set to continue until early next year. A spokesperson for SEIN commented on the positive results they've seen so far and the likelihood that this new treatment will be available soon. The FDA has yet to comment on the possibility of this controversial form of therapy being approved."

The report ended, Nina only managing to catch the last of it, and the anchor moved onto a reminder that it was flu season with a cheery voice that didn't quite match what she was talking about. Nina stopped paying attention at that point, instead recalling a conversation she'd had not so long ago. She remembered the smell of coffee and the way Ben had looked so tired as he sat across from her in a cozy little shop. Nina remembered him mentioning implanted memories being used in therapy and the protests he'd had to help control.

At the time, she hadn't thought much about it, despite the things she was dealing with. Maybe there had been too much going on, or maybe she just didn't want to believe that something like that had been done to her. Now though, Nina couldn't afford to dismiss things so easily. Not when she had memories she knew weren't hers—memories of a woman long dead—and a man sitting in prison thinking of people who he'd never known.

Someone must have implanted memories in us, but when? Nina asked herself as she stared blankly at the television screen. The coffee in her hand slowly cooled. And why doesn't Fearnley have the same memories as me?

That was something she was sure he would have mentioned. Fearnley had spoken about memories coming back to him, and then having two sets of memories about the same event. Perhaps, Nina thought, implanting memories hadn't worked as well as Alice—or whoever it was that had put those memories in Fearnley's head—had thought. There were still things that slipped through. Memories that should have been erased and others that never should have been placed in Fearnley's head in the first place.

"We don't have a daughter," Fearnley's ex wife had said. Nina believed her, she was a woman who had no reason to lie. Nina also believed Fearnley and the genuine heartbreak that had been present in his voice when he'd asked Nina to pass on a message to the daughter he remembered so fondly—so vividly.

He mentioned headaches.

Nina thought about the last conversation she'd had with the man, where he'd told her of the headaches he'd get when he thought of that day. The day Alice had died. Still, headaches were a common side effect to the procedure both Nina and Fearnley had gone through. She'd been told as much by the doctors, still got them at times. She recalled telling Nat as much, and felt a twinge of pain in her head at that very moment.

Nina might have dismissed the fleeting ache at any other time, but with Fearnley still on her mind, she wondered if maybe the memories of Alice weren't all that had been placed in her head. For the first time since she'd found out about Fearnley's false memories, Nina wondered if maybe he wasn't the only one living a lie.

No, I would know, she told herself. Fearnley had memory lapses. I would know.

The thought did little to comfort her when she knew all too well how easy it could be to get lost in something as fragile as memories. Fearnley hadn't suspected a thing about the memories of his daughter, and it had taken him far too long to realize his recollections of the night of Alice's death were flawed. His memories had begun to crumble at some point, but Nina's own recollections still felt whole with the exceptions of the ones Alice had clearly implanted.

So when did it all go wrong for him? Nina wondered, standing and abandoning her lukewarm drink on the coffee table.

She went in search of the notebook where she'd made notes during her conversations with Fearnley. After searching for a minute, Nina found what she was looking for. She'd written down as much as she could from what Fearnley told her during their phone call. Nina's meticulous notes didn't let her down.

Memories wrong, headaches when recalled, new memories days ago. After imprisonment, alt memories surfaced. The last bit had been added later, something Nina often did to make her notes clearer. Even without the note, it was obvious just how the memories implanted in Fearnley's head had finally fallen away to reveal the truth while Fearnley was in prison.

Could something have triggered it? Nina wondered, attempting to find a plausible reason for Fearnley's memories changing. Or did the memories just degrade naturally?

If that were true, then there was the possibility that Nina's own implanted memories would begin to falter sometime soon. After all, it had been some time since Alice had placed her own memories into Nina. Nina just wished she could know more about what happened to Fearnely while he was in Alice's care. What had been done to him and when each procedure had been performed would help Nina figure out when Fearnley's false memories had been implanted.

The problem was, Nina would need his medical records for that. With her resources being so limited, there was only one way she could get them, and that meant heading into the one place she did not want to go back to at the time.

Nina looked down at her notes, thought about that particular conversation with Fearnley. About how each day Fearnley spent in prison wore on the man's mind—scratching at it's already paper thin walls—and about Alice's gaze watching her expectantly. The look had changed just the slightest bit each time Nina saw it, until she thought she could see a silent plea shining within that green gaze. Those were things that Nina knew she couldn't ignore, and so she knew she had to act.

- - - - - - - - -

The memories of the last time Nina had been in the research center seemed like they belonged to a whole other lifetime. At least, Nina wished they did.

As soon as she stepped inside the building, there was a sense of unease that washed over her. The bright lights bounced off the spotless white floors, highlighting just how clinical the whole place was—how cold. It was a detail Nina had pushed out of her mind since she'd last been there. Perhaps because she'd wanted to forget she'd ever even had any need to step into the place.

Now, with each of her steps emitting a sharp note that seemed too loud to her own ears, Nina tried not to think about the way being in that place made her feel. She tried not to think about how her hands were shaking almost imperceptibly while her heart beat wildly inside her chest, setting a quick pace that echoed in her ears. Every gaze that settled upon her, every hushed conversation she passed by, made her heightened sense of awareness drive the paranoia she'd struggled to shove to the back of her mind for the time being.

No one knows you, Nina told herself, fighting back the urge to straighten the nursing smock she was wearing, one that had been surprisingly easy to find. No one knows you don't belong here.

She gave a woman—older and looking concerned enough that Nina figured she must have been visiting someone undergoing treatment—a smile that felt stiff on her face. It was a brittle thing that was near to cracking and falling apart under the weight of all that Nina carried. The moment she was out of view, the expression collapsed back into the tentatively neutral look Nina was keeping on her face. All of her doubts and fears along with the rush of nerves she felt were carefully kept locked inside while her face remained impassive.

Nina was still convinced she could feel eyes watching her, following her every move. Her steps never faltered, her gaze remained fixed ahead while her mind struggled with keeping Alice's memories back as they threatened to emerge. The pristine white hall flashed to a not so brightly lit one with cream colored walls. Nina blinked and the image in her mind changed.

Still, she kept a steady pace up until she made it to a door with a familiar name still displayed on it in neat, black lettering.

"Alice Cassill," Nina read softly, her eyes staring at the door for a moment, not surprised at the flash of a pale face staring back through a mirror. The image—a recurring memory that Nina had seen more times than she could count—barely registered as she peered through the slim strip of glass on the door.

The office had been stripped bare, something Nina had expected. Disappointment still settled heavily in the pit of her stomach as she thought of what she could have learned from Alice's belongings. Nina let out a soft sigh of resignation as her gaze swept over the empty office.

It was a small room, white walls contrasting with the dark grey carpet that looked to be new. The thought of why the flooring had been replaced crossed Nina's mind, making her stomach turn.

She took a step back at that, thinking of the reports she'd read, of how Alice had been found laying on her office floor in a pool of blood. Nina thought of the vivid green eyes staring at her and of how they might have been glazed over, unseeing even as they stared out of pale face. A wave of nausea overtook her, one Nina just barely managed to push back.

Once she'd gotten a hold of herself—once she no longer felt like she was fighting a losing battle against her emotions—Nina took a quick look around her. The hall was still empty, an unnatural sort of silence hovering over the place. Knowing she wouldn't find anything else there, she pulled out her phone.

Well before she'd entered the building, Nina had planned as much as she could given the circumstances. She'd managed to get a rough map of the building, the rest of the details and locations—like Alice's office—she knew from frequenting the place not so long ago. There was just one place she needed to make sure she knew the location to.

The filing room.

It was a not so short journey, one that would feel about a hundred times longer thanks to the nerves running through Nina's body at the moment. The room was a couple of floors down, in an area most often frequented by those who were employed by the research institute. Nina tried not to go over all of the things that could go wrong in that situation. Of how she had already taken much too long inside the building.

She could feel the cameras watching her, like unblinking eyes stalking her through the halls. It made her skin prickle and her eyes flicker around the place. Nina wanted to leave, wanted to rush out of the building and never look back. Somehow, she managed to remain in place, calmly sliding her phone back inside her pocket and taking the first of many steps down the hall.

Her breathing remained steady, a conscious effort on her part. It helped her focus on something other than what would happen if she were caught or the images of a hall with cream colored walls nearly as spotless as the one she was walking down at that moment that flashed in her head. Vivid visions that almost seemed to blend with reality.

Sooner than Nina had expected, she was standing in front of the elevators. Gleaming silver doors held her reflection. Nina turned her gaze to the ground until the doors finally slip open. She glanced up, catching sight of a couple of nurses dressed in a similar fashion as her and felt a knot of tension forming once again inside of her.

As she had from the moment she stepped foot inside the building, Nina pulled on a smile she hoped seemed sincere enough. Thankfully, the nurses were occupied with their own conversation. They returned her smile and nodded as they walked out.

Nina stepped inside, the doors closed and at last she was able to release a relieved sigh. She leaned against the cool steel wall and looked up at the numbers slowly changing, the seconds she spent inside the elevator feeling like a reprieve. That moment was gone when the doors opened just a second later, a floor away from Nina's destination, and a man walked in.

There was a swell of nerves as soon as she realized that someone was walking in, something that increased when Nina realized that she knew the man on the other side of the doors.

He was a doctor there, a relatively young one that she had sometimes seen around, but hadn't interacted with. Still, the thought that she—with her flawed memory—could recognize him made her wonder if he would as well.

For a moment, his eyes narrowed just the slightest bit, his gaze swept over Nina's face. She could almost see the gears turning in his head, struggling to place her face amidst all his memories while she recalled all the times she'd walked past him after her surgery, her father at her side as she hobbled down the hall. Nina remembered the detached interest in his eyes as he glanced her way. The moment was gone soon enough. He nodded—unable to see the same scarred patient from back then in the woman standing in front of him—stepped inside and Nina released the breath she'd unconsciously been holding.

After what felt like an eternity, the elevator reached the floor Nina would be getting off on. It was a conscious struggle to keep her steps at a normal pace when what she most wanted was to run out of the elevator. The doors closed behind her and relief washed over her even as she refused to look back.

Like Nina had expected, there was an increase in activity in the floor where the filing room was. Nurses walked by her, eyes roaming over patients' notes, others chatting with each other. Nina worked up a smile, a small one that still served to make everyone think she was at ease—that she was supposed to be there.

The walk to the filing room was a blur, most of Nina's attention occupied by the placid look she had to maintain on her face and the images of the hall from Alice's memories flooding into her mind. When she came back to herself, Nina was standing in front of the double doors that made up the entrance to the filing room. She could hear people walking around nearby, some chatting quietly, but the loudest thing was the sound of her heart pounding in her ears at the thought that behind that door could be the answers she so desperately needed.

Nina stretched out her hand to open the door, scars hidden beneath the cardigan she wore yet still there—always would be. The image of a child's hand, small and pale, flashed in her mind. A sunlit hall and a gleaming doorknob. The giggling of a child. Nina disregarded it all as she pushed open the doors and walked in.

The room was spacious, yet crammed with shelves upon shelves of files in the form of movable record cabinets. It was something that made Nina reconsider her idea as the task of finding a single file amongst all of the ones in front of her seemed more daunting a task than she had previously thought. There was still her fear of getting caught—of running out of time while she searched through all the files—something she pushed away as she strolled in. A quiet rustling nearby told her there was someone else in the room.

Nina ignored that in favor of finding what she was there for and getting out of there as soon as possible. That task was made difficult when she realized that she had no idea on how the files were organized. Each manila folder was coded with colors, numbers and letters. There was little labeling visible on the surface, and none of what Nina could see was remotely helpful in finding Fearnley's records.

She pulled out her phone, looked at the time and knew she'd spent too much time in there already. Nina knew she needed to leave and soon. From nearby, she could still hear the sound of papers being shuffled. For a minute, Nina stood there, eyes roaming over the overwhelming amount of files in front of her while the sounds of someone else searching through files seemed to grow louder. The clock was ticking, Nina heard steps heading towards the door. As much as she didn't want to, she knew what she had to do.

"Excuse me," she called out, heart pounding in her chest as the young male nurse stopped and turned towards her, a couple of folders in his grasp. "I was wondering if you could help me. I'm new and I've been asked to find some files." Nina did her best to appear apologetic for interrupting the man, letting just a hint of the nerves she felt slip through.

"Let me guess, having trouble figuring out the system?" the man said with an amused smile.

"Yeah, I guess I'm just a bit overwhelmed. First day nerves," she let out a laugh that was a bit relieved at having convinced the nurse. At least for the time being.

"It can be tough to get the hang of it. Took me about a week when I first started." Nina nodded while he spoke, all the while thinking of the seconds ticking away. "So, what are you looking for?"

Nina felt her smile widen just the slightest bit and could almost feel the files already within her grasp.

Chapter 15

The relief Nina felt as she left the building was nearly overwhelming. She still kept her pace steady as she marched out of the front doors with the files tucked under her arm. Nerves still simmered within her, bubbling up with each gaze she caught on her way out, each whispered conversation that her paranoia insisted was about her. As soon as she was out, Nina let out a breath, closing her eyes as the cool wind hit her face.

Even then, she didn't stop. Instead, she walked quickly to her car, not daring to look back. The cool handle of her car's door felt comforting—felt like safety. Nina climbed inside, tossing the files onto the passenger seat. She stared at them for a moment, feeling some disbelief at having actually pulled it off.

Admittedly, it hadn't been easy, and she was just fortunate that the man who'd helped her hadn't bothered to ask many questions. She just worried about the look he'd given her when she named Fearnley. Clearly, he knew who he was—knew what he had done. He'd still helped Nina find the records she needed before leaving the room.

After that, the rest was a blur. Maybe because Nina had been so focused on getting out. On not getting caught. On the answers that modest folder in her hands could hold. Now, sitting inside of her car with the dim light from stormy skies washing over them, the records seemed so simple—so insignificant. It was difficult to think of how much Nina had gone through to get them.

After a moment, Nina turned her gaze away, started the car, and drove home.

It was as Nina reached her home that her phone buzzed inside her pocket, a silent notice of a call that played over and over until it became clear Nina wouldn't answer. For a moment, Nina considered picking up, but thought better of it as she knew her friends would want to more than a quick conversation to know she was fine. They would want time Nina wasn't able to give them at the moment.

The phone stilled just as Nina parked. She wondered who it was calling her, and just as she pulled out her phone, it bussed once more to notify her of a message.

"Nat," Nina read the name displayed on her screen. She ignored the message for the time being, grabbed the files next to her and headed to her apartment.

As soon as she entered, Nina noticed the unsettling silence that had become so stifling as of late. It was something that had never bothered her before but now seemed like a prominent and unfortunate part of her life. Nina sometimes found herself wondering when she had managed to isolate herself so much.

She was reminded of the unread message in her phone and of all the calls she'd missed. Guilt flashed through her, and Nina found her hand going to her pocket, fingers curling around the phone she kept there. A wide smile flashed through her mind as a twinge of pain shot through her head, her hand sliding out of her pocket and up to reflexively touch her head. The pain was gone in an instant, along with Nina's desire to speak to anyone.

Instead, Nina walked over to the coffee table in her living room and dropped Fearnley's records on top of it before walking off to get changed. The feel of the clothes she had on reminded her of the nerves that had filled her when she was looking for Fearnley's files. It was something Nina didn't want to recall. Not when it made her feel so different from who she had been before—someone who searched for the truth without fearing it.

For what was far from the first time, and would certainly not be the last, Nina was reminded of all that was taken from her on the night of the accident. It was a memory that seemed so distant but no less significant.

The sky was streaked with pinks and purples marking the setting of the sun by the time Nina sat down and opened the records, the television tuned onto a show she'd never watched—a thriller that didn't seem half as crazy as her life. Her notepad was next to her along with a pen as was her usual cup of coffee. Nina already anticipated it being another long night. It was nothing new.

Fearnley's medical records were ordered chronologically, with the latest notes and files at the top. Nina decided if she wanted to get a good understanding as to what happened to the man, she'd have to start from the beginning. Nina ignored the sections she didn't think would be of use, at least for the time being. Perhaps it was because she wanted to get through it as quickly and efficiently as possible, or maybe it was just because she was fully aware of just how much she was invading Fearnley's privacy.

It's all necessary, she told herself, looking through the treatment plan that had been outlined for Fearnley.

A lot of it was much like what Nina had gone through. She still knew perfectly well what was written in her medical records—something she'd requested as soon as she could remember to do so. As Nina read along, moving onto the diagnosis the man had received, the similarities continued. It was all so like Nina's experience that she found herself thinking back on those difficult days in the hospital.

The strong smell of alcohol mixed with the scent of medication and the hushed whispers as her doctors spoke with her father. Those were constants during Nina's stay along with the pain—both physical and mental—that came from learning so much had changed. So many things had happened, things Nina would never remember. Nina had learned to cope with it all, with the uncertainty of what the future would hold for her.

Now it seemed that uncertainty had only increased.

Nina moved onto the progress notes, most of them written in small, neat lettering that flowed together along the page. It was the first time Nina had seen Alice's writing. She had been heavily involved with Fearnley's treatment, unlike with Nina's case where she had served as more of an adviser.

Why? What was different with our cases? Nina wondered. Whatever the reason was, Alice seemed to have distanced herself from that point of research. What changed?

Nina considered that, thought about what would make someone like Alice—someone deeply devoted and successful in her line of work, excited in the possibilities they could open up—seemingly lose interest.

No, not interest. Something else changed. Something made her step back. Nina kept that in mind. It was one more answer she would have to search for.

Her gaze returned to the notes before her. In them, Alice spoke about Fearnley making good progress after the surgery. The implant had steadily made it easier for the man to make long term memories. It was a gradual shift, something Nina vaguely remembered having gone through. Seeing it outlined in detail, despite the patient being someone else, was interesting. To Nina, it almost felt like a glimpse into her own past.

She still had the first memories she'd created after she'd received the implant—fragments that were embedded into Nina's mind. The brightly lit room where she'd recovered, the stench of disinfectant and intangible feeling of loss, though Nina wasn't sure at the time what it was that she had lost. Her father's hand in her own, a comforting touch that was still vivid in Nina's mind. It was something that had helped Nina get through her most difficult moments. She wondered if Fearnley had anyone to provide that for him. Not a moment later, she found the answer to that.

"Patient is in good spirits after call from former spouse. The support has had a marked effect on patient's progress." Nina didn't doubt that.

Fearnley's former wife had seemed like a kind woman. Kindness, Nina knew, could work wonders for those in need, and Fearnley had very much needed it.

Nina kept reading, much of the notes describing short memories that Fearnley had begun forming. They increased in frequency as time progressed, the memories themselves becoming longer, more detailed.

"Patient can recall in detail the conversation we had the previous day. He mentions a scent of rain and the flowers his former spouse sent to him."

Nina remembered the scent of flowers that had been present in some of Alice's memories, lavender and wildflowers. She shook her head and focused on the dark ink that seemed to blur as the cream colored hall flashed in her mind.

Not now, she thought, willing away the memories.

The ink in front of her blurred together, lines merging as her eyes struggled to focus and a headache began to form. Nina sat back, a hand reaching up to her head as her grasp on the records slackened. She closed her eyes, pressed them tight and hoped when she opened them the world had righted itself.

When the memories that weren't her own were no longer strug-gling to surface, Nina opened her eyes again. Her hands shook, slight tremors that she'd become used to. After a moment, she reached out for the coffee laying on the table, steam still rising from it, and took a sip. Nina savored the drink, strong and earthy taste still hot as it ran down her throat. She focused on it, on the way the fading light from the setting sun streamed in through the windows and the faint sounds of the city that drifted up into her apartment.

The mundane sights and sounds grounded her, made her feel steady in a world that felt like it was always tilting, trying to knock her off her feet. In that moment, everything was clear. Steady.

Nina breathed easy as the sounds from the television washed over the room and the scent of coffee—with it's bitter taste still in her mouth—stuck in her mind. She wondered if she'd remember any of it as vividly the next day.

"Smell, sights and sounds may all act as triggers for memories." The quote emerged from some part of her brain that had worked to store as much information as possible.

Alice knew that. She'd seen it with Fearnley, the way he remem-bered sensory details. Nina thought. So she made sure to include those when she planted her memories, when she constructed them.

Now, Nina found herself wondering when Alice had done all of that. She'd taken the time to create new memories, strong ones that would be almost painfully vivid. And then she had stuck them inside Fearnley.

"Great, now I just need to figure out when," Nina muttered.

She turned the page after skimming through the rest, her eyes growing tired as they scanned the notes. Fearnley's progress was steady, Alice praised it enough in the notes that Nina could tell she truly cared about her patient. She also seemed happy to have Fearnley's ex wife providing support, though Nina wasn't sure if that wasn't mostly because it seemed to help with Fearnley's recovery. One thing Nina noted, was that there was no mention of the daughter he still thought he had. She wondered if that would change as the notes progressed.

Alice's notes were meticulous, pointing out every change—however slight it was—that emerged during Fearnley's treatment. Every new memory that was formed and relayed to Alice, every visit and call that Fearnley received, every headache and bad dream. All of it was carefully noted down in Alice's neat writing. Nina was yawning by the time that changed.

The shift was sudden, but obvious enough that Nina noticed it right away. Alice's writing changed to a larger, slightly messier script, the letters wider and notes more impersonal. Nina felt her brow furrow, the corners of her lips tilting down just the slightest bit as her eyes swept over the new writing.

It's someone else's writing, Nina thought. Someone else took over Fearnley's care. Nina looked at the date, thinking about the timeline she'd written with what little she knew until then. She could rule out Alice's death, that was still some time away.

Nina turned a couple of pages, knowing it was near the end of the progress notes. Then, suddenly, Alice was back. Her careful writing stood out to Nina, who'd been poring over her notes for hours.

"Patient seems well, no unusual changes from when I last saw him."

Nina thought that was an odd way to word it. It was almost like Alice didn't know what she would find when she saw Fearnley.

And where did she go? Nina wondered.

Alice's absence had been a short one, perhaps just a couple of days. She'd still expected something to have changed upon her return, and Nina couldn't help but note the relief that seemed to be present in her written words.

Alice's notes went on for a couple more pages, and then they switched to the same messier writing when she was so clearly replaced. Nina looked at the date and felt her heart sink. The date was the day after Alice's death—the day Fearnley had walked back into the building where Alice had been murdered.

Nina sat back, a wave of sadness sweeping over her for reasons she couldn't quite identify. She wasn't certain if it was because Alice, a woman she'd hardly known, had died. Or if it was because it made her think back to the man still locked away in prison, with memories that weren't his own and a mind that was almost as close to shattering as Nina's.

She was drawn out of her thoughts by the sound of her phone vibrating on the coffee table. Without thinking, she grabbed it and nearly picked up the call, wincing immediately as she realized what she'd almost done in her distracted state. Instead of answering, she looked down at the name on the screen and was a bit surprised to see it was Nat.

Nina had already had several missed calls and messages from her friend that day. Enough that she considered picking up, especially given the late hour.

She's probably just worried, Nina told herself as the phone finally stilled, yet another missed called added.

She stared at the screen for a second longer, yawning and deciding it was time for her to get some rest. As she made her way to her room, Nina ignored the guilt she felt as she thought of her friends attempting to get in contact with her. More than that, Nina did her best to not think about the odd sense that something was wrong—that something was going on, something she was missing. After one last glance back to her phone, Nina headed off to bed, telling herself that she'd call her friend the next day.

That night, Nina dreamed. It wasn't the normal dreams she'd had before and neither was it the usual memories from Alice replaying in her head. She was back in the hall, the walls painted the same cream color as always and a scent of rain and earth and something that Nina—or perhaps it was Alice—could only register as familiar.

She took small steps, the world around her feeling all too large and the door at the end towering above her even from a distance. The picture on the wall hung high above her head as she passed it by without even pausing and then the door was in front of her. A small hand reached out, fingers almost touching the shining doorknob.

"Alice," a voice called, warm and affectionate. Nina turned, heart fluttering, and a single word flowed through her mind.

Mom.

Before Nina could fully turn, a laugh bubbling up through lips that were not her own, the world blurred and faded away along with the silhouette of a woman Nina had never known.

It was still early when Nina woke up. The sun was just starting to peek over the horizon, warm rays of light illuminating the world through grey clouds. Nina awoke to the now usual feeling of exhaustion which only became worse when she thought about all that was wrong in the world. It was enough to make her want to stay in bed, hiding from truths she didn't want to face and denying the wetness in her eyes as the images from the memories refused to fade.

But this time, there was also a sense of comfort, and a sadness that had been absent for longer than Nina could tell. The dull ache of a loss that was too great and the feeling that she knew who was calling Alice's name in that odd memory—that she knew where that cream colored hall was. The sense of familiarity, of comfort, was enough to make Nina certain.

Nina thought she knew where Alice had gone during Fearnley's treatment, when she'd left him to someone else's care and returned with the expectation that things would be different. Alice had left with the knowledge that something was wrong.

With much effort, Nina got up and began to get ready for the day. Coffee was brewed and a cup was drunk before she glanced at her phone, still sitting on top of the coffee table along with Fearnley's records and Nina's notes. On the television, the weatherman spoke with a voice too cheerful for such an early hour.

"There is a possibility of flash floods later this evening, with rain starting as early as noon in some parts." He wore a wide smile on his face as he gestured to the map behind him. Nina felt a twinge of pain that faded quickly enough that she wondered if she'd imagined it. The image of a crimson smile that had flashed in her head faded away slowly, but the thought of it gave Nina a feeling of unease.

She was distracted from both her musings and the smiling man on the television screen by the sudden sound of her phone vibrating from its place on top of the table. Nina reached for it immediately, before pausing to look at the name displayed on the screen.

"Ben," she said, surprised that he'd call so early. After a moment of hesitation, during which she recalled the guilt she'd felt the previous night after ignoring Nat's calls, she picked up. Before Nina could say anything, Ben spoke, voice sounding rushed—desperate.

"Nina, what did you do?"

The words took Nina aback, that feeling of wrongness from the previous night returning like a wave slamming onto the shore. Ben was worried, anxious and Nina knew whatever he had to say couldn't be good.

Things were changing, and Nina hoped she was ready.

Chapter 16

Nina wasn't sure what to make of Ben's sudden message. She stood there, brow furrowed and lips slightly parted as she processed the words he'd just spoken, trying to figure out why it was that he sounded so desperate, or what he thought she'd done. The abrupt message had been enough to throw Nina off balance.

"What do you mean? What's going on, Ben?" Nina asked, doing her best to remain calm even as her heartbeat quickened at the urgent tone of Ben's voice.

"Listen, I don't have a lot of time," Ben went on, voice quiet and as close to calm as he could manage at the time. There was still a tenseness in his voice that was clear as day to Nina, who'd known Ben for so long. "I need you to be honest with me, please. Did you go to the SEIN building yesterday?"

Nina felt her brow rise, eyes widening at Ben's question. Her mind quickly assessed her options, thinking of whether she should tell Ben the truth. Maybe if he hadn't sounded so desperate, Nina might have lied, might have told Ben she hadn't been in the building since her last checkup weeks ago—something that felt more like an eternity after all that had happened. Instead, she knew she had to be honest with him, knew that all he'd ever wanted was to help and that likely hadn't changed. Nina trusted Ben.

"I did," she said simply, not knowing what else to tell Ben or whether she should elaborate. Nina figured it would be best to let Ben lead the conversation until she knew what was going on. She ignored the unease that had risen up inside of her from the moment Ben had first spoken.

"Damn it," Ben muttered a curse and Nina felt her heart sink as she knew she wouldn't like what Ben had to say. "Nina, what did you do?"

"What's going on?" Nina asked instead of answering. "How did you know I was there yesterday?"

"You were caught on camera." The words were enough to make Nina feel like everything around her had fallen away. The world felt unusually still and silent, with only Ben's voice audible to her ears. "There was a complaint about you, they said you broke in and took some records. Things you weren't supposed to have access to. Listen, I don't know what's going on or what you're up to, but you have to come clean and fast. Turn yourself in. Tell them the truth, whatever that is."

Ben's voice was steady, something Nina knew he was struggling to maintain. She was much in the same situation. Even as she fought to keep her breathing steady, Nina could feel her hands shaking ever so slightly as her mind betrayed her once again.

For just a moment, Nina was back in that pristine hall with the too bright lights and the overwhelming stench of disinfectant hanging around her like a thick fog—stifling. Unseen eyes seemed to follow her every move, making a shiver run up her spine as Nina did her best not to run from the building. Each step she took felt like too great a feat, the sound of them bouncing off the walls, deafening in the near silent white halls that melted off into cream colored walls with the scent of earth and spices.

"Nina." Ben's voice broke Nina out of her thoughts. She was startled, nearly dropping the phone as she came back to herself, but somehow managing to keep a grip on the slim device.

Her hands were shaking violently, the chaotic memories still clinging to the edges of her mind. She did her best to gather her thoughts and calm her racing heart. Ben was still waiting for whatever answers Nina could give him.

"I had to do it," Nina said without thinking. "There were things I needed to know, and there was no other way," she went on as she heard Ben curse.

"What kind of records did you take?" Nina hesitated before deciding it was in her best interest to be honest with Ben. He'd find out the truth soon enough either way.

"Christopher Fearnley's," she said, and could hear a sharp intake of breath from the other end of the line. "I took Fearnley's medical records." The admission was enough to silence Ben, if only for a second.

"What are you looking into? And be honest this time."

Nina took a deep breath, braced herself for what would come next. As much as she trusted Ben, she wasn't sure he trusted her at the moment. Still, there was no way she could hide everything from him. Just as there was no way she could tell him all that she knew. Not yet.

"I can't explain to you right now, and I don't think I have time to, but I don't think Fearnley is guilty. He was framed by someone, and I think it has something to do with SEIN and the treatment he underwent there. That's why I needed his records."

"You can't be serious," Ben muttered, and Nina didn't think it was particularly pointed at her. "They think you're working with him, I don't know why, but they think something's going on. You visited him in prison, lied about it being for work so you could get an interview. You even spoke to his ex wife with the same excuse even though you haven't gone back to work yet. They checked, you haven't been back to work since the accident." There was a reproach there, but more than that, there was hurt. Ben was hurt to know Nina had lied to him.

She swallowed back the guilt she felt at that. There was no time to regret choices she could no longer change. Now, she knew why Ben was so anxious. The situation was more serious than Nina had first thought. She knew she had to move.

Nina began gathering all of the notes and documents scattered around into a messy stack while still on the phone. Her mind—for the time being—was focused on the task at hand.

"What do they want, to question me about the files I took? About Fearnley?"

"I don't know," Ben said after some hesitation, and Nina could tell that he simply didn't think it best to tell her.

"Are they on their way now?" she asked. Nina knew there was no use in trying to tell Ben everything. There was simply too much to say and the clock was ticking.

"Not yet. I called as soon as I heard, but they'll leave any minute now." He sighed and Nina could just imagine him rubbing the bridge of his nose. "If you really think he's innocent then turn yourself in. Let them question you and tell them what you know. Don't make things any worse than they already are."

Nina could have laughed at that. Just the thought of trying to explain to the cops—to anyone—the connection between her, Alice and Fearnley was enough to make Nina grimace. It was the kind of thing that no one would believe. Not with only half formed theories and the memories of a dead woman in Nina's mind as evidence.

"I can't," Nina said, and even to her own ears it sounded like an apology. "Ben, I can't give up now, and the things I know, I don't think anyone would believe it. Not now. I need to know the truth—all of it—first."

"Then I'll help you. I swear. You know I always will, but you can't do anything to make things worse. Nina, you can't run."

She felt her mouth quirk up into a half smile. Ben knew her too well. He should have known there was no use in asking that of her.

"Why did you call me, Ben?" she asked, voice soft.

"I don't know. Maybe I just wanted to find out what's going on from you, because I trusted you to be honest with me at least. And I trusted you to do the right thing."

"Then you shouldn't have called."

"Nina—"

"Bye, Ben. And thank you." Nina hung up before Ben could say anything else and shut off the device.

She felt a knot of nerves forming in the pit of her stomach, the reality of the situation still not fully sinking in. It was too much to take for a mind as fractured as hers. And so, Nina pushed it all back, focused on nothing but what was in front of her. Focused on the need to leave as soon as possible.

For what felt like hours, but were really only a couple of short minutes, Nina rushed around her apartment gathering everything she needed. All of the notes and records she had on Alice and Fearnley were tucked away inside a bag along with as much cash as Nina could find. All the while, Nina avoided looking at the clock. Already her hands were shaking, her heart pounding as she shot nervous looks towards the door as she kept packing all she thought she'd need.

The small bag she had packed felt like a heavy burden as she hoisted it up onto her shoulder.

Nina refrained from breathing a sigh of relief as she pulled on a coat and finally walked out of the apartment. After all, she wasn't in the clear just yet.

Nina threw one last look back at her home. She looked at the bare walls where photos had once been and didn't feel nearly as sad as she should have at the possibility that she wouldn't see the place for a long while. The truth was that the place hadn't felt like home for a while.

Not when everywhere she looked there were memories she didn't want to recall, triggers that drove her back to that cream colored hall with the scent of spices and earth heavy in the air. It was also where she'd finally felt like her life was coming together, all those years ago when she'd just started her career. It was where a picture of her mother had hung on the wall before the sight of it had been too much for her shattered mind.

The memories she had of the place clashed against each other. Moments Nina would always treasure were tainted by those she wished she could lock away forever. All Nina could do now was move on.

After what felt like too long a moment, Nina hitched her bag up higher onto her shoulder, the weight of it lighter than all that bore down on her mind. A hint of petrichor hung in the air even as sunlight—warm and inviting—streamed in through the windows. The place still felt stifling, and Nina felt what could only be relief as she finally turned away from it all.

The door shut behind her, and Nina didn't look back again.

Chapter 17

Rain was just beginning to fall—so weak it was barely there—when Nina walked into the dimly lit room where she would be spending the night. Off white walls looked nearly yellow beneath the dull lighting while the few pieces of furniture looked worn even from the doorway. Nina didn't mind it so much. She wouldn't be staying for long, not if she could help it, and the place was desolate enough that it would not be easy to find.

No one would be looking for her there. At least, that was what Nina was counting on.

She sighed as she closed the door behind her, making sure to lock it before walking to the bed and dropping her bag on top of the tacky, multi-colored bedding. Even with the bed looking like a far cry from the one in her apartment, it looked incredibly enticing to Nina at the moment. She was exhausted, her eyes burning while a headache built up and everything that had happened filled her mind to the brim until Nina could no longer process it all. Simply put, Nina didn't know what to do.

For someone who'd always been so self assured, so certain of her role and her purpose, that was a frightening feeling. It was something Nina had been battling with, perhaps from the moment she awoke in a hospital bed with no memory of how she got there, something she'd managed to push back as she worked to get back to her normal life. And then, just as she managed to get a grip on who she was, it slipped away and she fell into a world that kept shifting beneath her feet—throwing her off balance.

Nina didn't know what to do, hadn't known for longer than she cared to consider, but she knew that simply sitting around—giving up—wasn't an option.

She took a deep breath, exhaled, and felt her head clear just a bit. Enough that she thought she could function well enough to do something. Even so, she dug around her bag for the emergency meds she carried and downed a couple of pills for the headache that was slowly becoming a real nuisance. Once that was done, she reached for the files she'd hurriedly packed away, pulling them out and making her way over to the desk across the small room.

The sole chair she was provided with was dragged back over the grey carpet that had seen better days. It creaked as Nina took a seat, the wood feeling flimsy enough that Nina was concerned about it giving away for a minute, but she settled down soon enough and opened up the files once more.

Perhaps there wasn't much more for Nina to find in there. Still, there was a certain comfort to be gained from doing something. Nina needed a purpose at that moment, something to guide her and show her what she should do when all the walls were closing in on her and the world felt like a stifling place. Something to drown out the voice telling her that she was going mad.

Nina found some of that in going through Fearnley's records, even if it was the second time.

The clock, an antiquated thing that reminded her of her school days, when she'd sat at an uncomfortable desk with a test in front of her and the ticking of the clock a steady warning that her time was slipping away. That very feeling returned to her in full at that moment. Behind her, the clock was ticking away, echoing in her mind as she tried to put all of her attention into the words on the pages before her. All the while, the conversation she'd had with Ben played over and over in her head.

I was so stupid, Nina couldn't help but think. *I shouldn't have gone back to that place.*

Her return to the SEIN building had felt like a mistake from the start, but Nina had credited that to purely personal reasons. After all, there was much reason for her to feel apprehensive about entering the building. The time she spent there after the accident was not something she wanted to be reminded of.

The clock on the wall kept ticking away and the words began to blur into a dark, inky mess. More than ever before, Nina wished she had someone she could talk to. Even if she hadn't gotten rid of her phone at some random point between her apartment and the distant motel she'd stumbled across after driving without a set course, Nina knew that there was no one she could confide in. Her friends, her family, couldn't be involved in the mess she'd trapped herself in. Ben had already done more than he should have by warning her.

Nina thought of Iris and Nat, and what they would think when they found out she'd left town—that the police were looking for her. She thought of her father, who'd already been through more than enough. The last time she'd seen him they'd walked out into the warm sunlight and cool wind, both feeling like a blessing after she'd been stuck indoors while recovering. He'd been worried then, and rightly so, but Nina had done her best to be strong. Now, she found it harder to do when she had no one to be strong for.

At that moment, a memory surfaced in her mind, one that Nina was no longer certain was her own. A warm presence, the laughter of a child bubbling up, and the feeling of a familiar presence that could only be described as comforting.

Mom, Nina thought, the word appearing in her mind unbidden. She thought of the smiling image of her mother that had once hung on the wall of her home. More than anything, Nina thought of all the times she'd sought out her mother for reassurance and the ease with which she'd been given it. Now, Nina wondered once more if maybe Alice hadn't done the same thing at a time when—for reasons still unknown to Nina—she had needed someone to be there for her.

She knew something was wrong, that's why she left Fearnley's treatment to someone else, Nina thought, searching amongst the mess of notes she'd hastily gathered for the rough timeline she'd worked out. So she went home. Went to her family. But what did she know and why did she leave? Was it really just to ease her mind?

It was her best guess, but it still seemed wrong. Alice seemed like a pragmatic person. She was, from what Nina could gather, direct and independent. It was difficult to think of her going home for something as simple as some familiar comfort in a time of need, not when something was bothering her so deeply about the work she was doing. Especially not while she worked with a patient like Fearnley, someone in whose progress she was so invested.

Unless that was why she left. Maybe something happened, something that made her distance herself from her work for a short while. Nina recalled Alice not being as involved in her own case. When she thought about it, that seemed peculiar. It would have been a good opportunity to see the effects of her work.

Nina leaned back in her seat, the chair creaking once again though this time the sound went ignored. Her brow was furrowed, a slight frown on her face and a far off look in her eyes as she lost herself in her thoughts.

Something drove her home, something related to her work. Nina decided that was the best trail of thought to follow at the moment. There was a chance that if she found out what it was that made Alice leave her work behind the whole puzzle would come together.

"Pull the right thread and the whole thing will unravel." Once again, the old piece of advice came back to Nina. *I just hope this is the right thread.*

What little of the weak sunlight that made it through the thick storm clouds and filtered in through the narrow space between the curtains was quickly fading. Night was still a ways off, but Nina didn't feel comfortable driving around just yet. Besides that, she didn't know where she would go next, her mind not being made up about what her next step would be, not with all of the uncertainties she was surrounded with at the time.

With that, Nina turned back to the records in front of her and the neatly written notes Alice had jotted down. Outside, the rain strengthened gradually until it became a downpour. The sound of the rain beating against the ground was a steady, almost soothing sound. It cut through the bleak silence Nina found herself in.

She eyed the small television set in her room, and finally decided to turn it on. The sounds of one of the many procedural shows flooded the room and made Nina feel a little less tense. As had become a habit, she left it on, despite not caring for the show.

Nina let out a yawn as she read on, getting to the end of Alice's notes and to the part written in unfamiliar handwriting. Fearnley's last visit had been short, according to the records. It had been a simple check up, he'd been doing well, the headaches that had plagued Nina as well being the only things that Fearnley had complained about. As Nina had been, Fearnley was reassured, told it was a normal side effect. He was sent home. Just days later, Fearnley turned himself in.

And then his memories changed. That was what Fearnley had said when they'd last spoken. His memories had changed, slowly at first—like they were eroded with time, the pieces fracturing until the truth broke free from the lies that were built around it. But then, at what point had those lies been placed in the man's head. When, and why, had someone made him think he had a daughter?

Was it while Alice was away? Nina thought, then recalled the first thing Alice had noted when she returned and saw her patient once again. No, she was looking for anything that could be off. She would have noticed, and Fearnley would have mentioned his daughter.

Nina dug out the notepad where she'd written down everything she'd found out while asking around about Fearnley. Notes on their conversations were also there, and it took Nina only a minute to find what she was looking for—the point where Fearnley had told her about the Night Alice was killed.

He said the memories came to him slowly, and the old ones—the ones that were implanted—were still there. What if those memories appeared gradually too? If he turned himself in days after Alice was killed, then the implanted memories probably didn't appear until later. Fearnley had, after all, said his memories of the incident were foggy when he'd first spoken to Nina. Now, Nina knew that it was entirely possible that was due to the memories slowly taking hold in Fearnley's mind.

They'd gone from fragments of sounds and images Fearnley could hardly put together to memories so vivid he was convinced of his own guilt. It was that guilt that drove Fearnley to confess, not being able to live with the thought of what he'd done. What he'd been framed for.

Now, Nina was back to needing to find out what it was that had driven Alice to leave her work and what connection that had to her murder.

What did she know? Nina asked herself, staring at the pages in front of her as if they held all the answer. And maybe they did, maybe Nina just wasn't looking in the right place.

She flipped through the pages, brow furrowed and energy all but gone. The sun was gone, the last rays of light having faded behind the horizon while the rain had slowed if only for a while. Nina glanced up at the closed door and considered heading out, if only for a moment. She did, after all, need food.

Since she'd left home, Nina hadn't felt so hungry. She'd been too preoccupied with all the things that had happened, things she hadn't fully processed. Between Ben's warning, the news that she was suspected of working with Fearnley, and the stress of her mind trying to hold itself together Nina hadn't felt anything but anxiety. Even at that moment, she wasn't particularly hungry, but she figured she should get something while she had the chance. After all, she couldn't be sure of what the next day would bring. It felt like she hadn't been sure of that for a long time.

A minute later, Nina cautiously opened the door to her room. The hall was empty, yellow lights illuminating the length of it and the air feeling cold and still with the scent of rain hanging heavily. Nina could see her breath, a white puff that dispersed in a second while her face began to prickle with the cold.

It was always colder outside the city, especially closer to the mountains. Nina wasn't so far from them, perhaps having sought out the most remote place instinctually. In a way, she was glad for that. The silence and peace helped keep her calm and, for the first time, she realized she'd yet to be caught in any of Alice's memories.

She tried not to think about that, maybe out of fear that those memories would emerge, as if summoned from the darkest corner of her mind. Instead, Nina focused on heading down the hall, towards the vending machines she'd seen when she'd arrived.

It was a short walk, the machines visible from just outside her room. Her shoes clicked against the ground in a way that nearly took her back to the hall with the pictures on the wall and the scent of earth and spices. She closed her eyes, took a deep breath, and thought about the theories she'd come up with regarding Fearnley and Alice. Nina thought about her conversation with Ben and whether the police would give up on her.

Probably not, she thought, wondering how serious the accusations against her were. Nina wished Ben had been able to tell her more. Still, he'd risked enough already, now she just hoped he was okay.

Before she knew it, Nina found herself standing before the vending machines. A bright selection of junk food was displayed in front of her in bright packaging. She nearly cringed at the thought sight of all the sweets and was only too glad there was a single vending machine selling soup. Nina would freely admit to having survived of of cup noodles for most of her college years. It was, after all, a stable of the college diet. She figured it was better than nothing.

"At least it's hot," she muttered, waiting for the hot water to fill the cup.

The warmth was pleasant as she picked it up and headed back to her room. She hadn't realized just how cold she was until her stiff fingers wrapped around the styrofoam cup. The familiar smell of the cheap condiments and the scent of rain still lingering in the air was soothing in a way. It reminded her of nights curled up on a lumpy bed, studying for some test and wondering when she'd have time to call her parents. The nostalgia was enough to keep Nina's mind from going to places she'd rather not visit. She was thankful for that much.

Nina was glad the moment she walked back into her room, not only because of the warmth the room provided. She sat at her desk with the meager meal she'd gathered and looked back to the notes and documents she'd been going over for what felt like the hundredth time. The clock on the wall was still ticking away and it reminded her of how skewed her sense of time had become as of late. Already her trip to retrieve Fearnley's files seemed like a distant memory.

She flipped the pages of Fearnley;s records, scanning the parts she'd not looked at as closely the first time around while her soup cooled at her side. The television was now showing an infomercial for some new piece of cookware, the type Nina's mother would have rushed out to buy as soon as she laid eyes on it.

Mom. The word resonated in some part of her mind along with a child's laughter and the name of a dead woman spoken in a warm tone. Nina raised a hand to her head, willing away the memories.

On the television, a woman prattled on about the product with a wide smile on painted lips while pain shot through Nina's skull and crimson smile flashed in her mind's eye. She closed her eyes, wondered if the shock was wearing off. If her mind would once again start to crumble.

"Stop it," she said in a harsh whisper, and asked herself who she was speaking to. Alice was gone, after all. There was nothing more she could do about the memories in Nina's mind.

The memories subsided, slowly slipping away until they were nothing but a distant presence inside of Nina's mind. With shaking hands, she picked up the files she'd been going over, intent on keeping busy.

Nina read carefully through a list of medications Fearnley was taking, the scheduled therapy sessions, the many check ups he'd received. It was all painfully mundane. At least, it was to Nina, who'd gone through much of the same after receiving a neuroprosthesis of her own. Her soup was consumed, the woman on the television had been replaced by a far less enthusiastic anchorwoman talking about some protests.

The serious, matter of fact way the news were delivered made it harder and harder for Nina to keep her eyes open. Exhaustion was catching up to her and Nina was struggling to keep going. She was starting to wish she had some coffee around.

Nina sat back, staring at the files she'd scanned more than once already, knowing she'd found as many answers as she was likely to find. There was still much Nina needed to know, but for that, she had to look at the big picture, she had to look at who was behind the treatment both her and Fearnley understood. Someone was pulling the strings, and now that Nina had a better idea of what was going on, she needed to find out who and why.

She closed the records, setting them aside for the time being, and pulled her laptop closer. SEIN had a public site, one that spoke about how much good they were doing in the medical community. One that Nina's father had looked at with hope. It was a sentiment that Nina might have shared at one time.

Nina felt a sense of bitterness towards it now, as she looked at images of smiling people on the front page. The usual welcoming homepage that greeted her was almost laughable, but she ignored it in favor of searching for information on the people working for the research institute. There was a long list, several with pictures of smiling doctors, researchers and nurses. Each had a short bit of information, mostly about their credentials and past achievements, but what Nina was really interested in was what projects they were currently working on.

Trials for neuroprosthetics—particularly hippocampal implants of the same sort both Nina and Fearnley had received—were still being conducted. But then, there was a more controversial project. One that Nina had disregarded for a long time, too preoccupied with everything that had been going on as of late. Memory implants.

Ben had mentioned it to Nina once, while they sat in a cafe with hot drinks. It had been a rare moment of peace that Nina now missed dearly. Now, Nina wished she'd asked more questions. It was too late for regrets.

One by one, Nina looked over each name listed in alphabetical order, jotting down the names of those connected to either the memory implants or the neuroprosthetics. Her list grew longer and longer with each passing minute, the ticking of the clock on the wall a steady marker of the flow of time, something Nina had lost track of since nightfall. Outside, the rain had picked up once more, and by the time Nina had gotten to the names under the letter R, the rain had become a full on downpour.

Even inside, there was a chill in the air that had Nina wishing once again for a hot drink. She debated going outside to get more soup, but decided against it. The short walk down the hall had been difficult enough the first time around. Instead, Nina draped her jacket over her shoulders and continued to stare at the screen with tired eyes.

As the moved farther and farther away past midnight, it became increasingly more difficult for Nina to keep her eyes open, her eyelids feeling heavy and her thoughts becoming muddled as sleep fought to overtake her.

Not yet, she thought, willing herself to stay awake.

It was becoming more and more difficult to focus on what it was that she was reading, the words blurred and refusing to register. Several times, she found herself being forced to stop just to go over something once again.

That all changed with a single image of a smiling woman.

The moment Nina saw it, she felt more awake than she had since she'd spoken to Ben that morning—something that still felt like it had happened years earlier. Her eyes widened, the pen she'd somehow managed to keep a grip on finally slipping from her hand to hit the desk with a weak clattering sound. For that moment, the world seemed to still, the ticking of the clock, the rain beating against the pavement outside and the voices streaming through the television all fading as Nina focused on the picture she couldn't tear her eyes away from.

Nat. The name stuck out in her mind as she looked at the woman who, without a doubt Nina had called her childhood friend. A woman who worked at a law firm and was supposed to know nothing of the medical field.

And yet, there she was, her eyes sharp as always amidst pale skin and a crimson smile stretching across her face. It was a smile that had once seemed warm to Nina—comforting. Now, as she looked upon it with a sinking feeling in her stomach, it seemed like a smug, mocking gesture. Those mismatched eyes, that sharpness she'd taken for cleverness taking on a dangerous glint, stared straight at her.

Nina suddenly found herself standing, her chair toppling over with a sound that felt too loud. She stared at that smiling face and felt a sharp pain shoot through her head. Even as she closed her eyes, gripping her head with a shaking hand, that crimson smile flashed through her head. And then, perhaps not so strangely, she thought of Fearnley.

"I'd get these headaches when I thought about that day. . ." he'd said, when he spoke about memories that weren't really his. Right before he'd asked Nina to pass on a message to a daughter he had never even had.

No, I know who I am, Nina told herself, even as her memories crumbled around her, the lies that had been stuck inside her head falling to pieces as the truth emerged. The pain in her head grew with every passing second as did the pain in her heart as she thought of the things she'd lost and the things that were still being stolen from her.

Warm summer days spent playing with a friend. Shared laughter and the feel of a hand as small as her own in her grasp. Mismatched eyes that smiled at her from a friend's face. It was all a lie that Nina had held close to her heart.

A broken past that had never existed.

The world spun around her as the rain roared outside and the ticking of the clock seemed like a deafening sound that stook out from the chatter on the television. Nina's head pounded and her eyes stung even as she pressed them tightly closed, the cold wetness of tears running down her face.

The world fell away and Nina's consciousness went with it.

Chapter 18

The room was cold and dark when Nina opened her eyes. A chill seeped into her very bones as she lay on the floor, staring blankly up at the off-white ceiling. Outside, the rain persisted, while the clock on the wall continued to tick away the minutes. Both remained unchanged. The same could not be said for Nina.

Something inside her felt different, yet one more piece of who she was—or who she thought she was—having broken off. Nina had picked up the pieces once. Put them back together until she was whole again, despite the cracks still visible to those who cared to look. She didn't think she could manage that a second time.

Not when he thought back to all that she'd learned the previous night. Crimson lips stretched in a mocking smile, and Nina had to push the thought away as she felt a surge of pain in her head.

Slowly, she sat up, her back aching almost as much as her head and her body feeling stiff from having spent so long lying on the floor. Dawn hadn't yet broken, cool moonlight filtering through the slim gap between the curtains, and Nina felt an odd sense of disorientation at not knowing just how late it was, or for how long she'd been lying on the worn carpet of the motel room.

That feeling grew stronger as her weary mind struggled to catch up with all that had happened. Ben's warning to her, the long drive without a destination, a familiar face that she'd never truly known—it all mixed into a muddled mess that Nina was caught in the midst of. And yet, the greatest detail Nina fought to understand was Nat. Or at least, the woman she'd thought Nat was.

The woman who Nina could still picture as a young girl, smiling brightly as she walked at Nina's side. A blue backpack rested on her shoulders with the small rabbit ornament Nina had gifted her months earlier dangling from it. Nina could still remember the way they'd head home together, both of the girls living on the same street.

She remembered snacking on apple slices and yogurt cups at a wide, wooden table in Nat's brightly lit kitchen. The way the sun would gleam off the pristine counters and the feel of the warm, summer breeze as it blew through the kitchen window, rustling the pages of printout that made up the girls' homework. Nina remembered it all, remembered the feeling of happiness—of acceptance—that came with having a friend like Nat.

Most of all, Nina remembered the day she thought she'd lost all of that. It was with perfect clarity that Nina could recall the way the sun's rays had seemed so feeble as they streamed through thick clouds in thin strips, breaking through the dullness of the day. She could see how the light bounced off the shards of glass scattered over the asphalt, like stars glimmering amidst a pitch black sky.

The scent of petrichor hung thickly in the air, water pooling all around her and the faint coolness of drizzle just starting to dot her skin. There were cries of help, of panic, of emotions Nina couldn't be bothered to identify at the time. Not when her own heart threatened to beat out of her own chest and a sense of dread mixed with horror rose inside of her. From the distance, there was the sound of sirens, the wailing sound seeming like a mournful cry to Nina's ears as it grew closer.

Amidst it all, was Nat, the only source of stillness in the chaos that surrounded them. Crimson stained her clothes, her face, and Nina was almost glad she couldn't see her friend's state from where she stood, shaking from more than the chill in the air.

And then, she was in a startlingly white waiting room. The stench of antiseptic Nina would someday come to detest was almost stifling as she sat next to her mother, who had an arm still wound tightly around her. Nina remembered the exhaustion, the dread, as she waited for news on her friend.

When she finally did see Nat again, much later, she was met with a pair of mismatched eyes. The smile on Nat's face was sharp as Nina stared into those eyes, gleaming a they stared at her, and the thought of them—the memory Nina had always thought belonged to her—was enough to make her shiver.

The memories were vivid, so much so that Nina could almost convince herself that they were true. That such a large part of her life wasn't a lie. She wished she were able to do that to herself. Nina wished she could believe the way that Fearnley did.

"I know who I am." The words Nina had repeated to herself not so long ago played over in her head, mocking her. Reminding her that she didn't know anything after all.

The thought nearly drew a bitter laugh from her. She remembered Fearnley, sitting in a cell with only the thought of the daughter he didn't have to serve as comfort and of the way she'd pitied a man living a lie.

"It's her birthday next week." Fearnley has confided in Nina with a broken tone.

"We don't have a daughter."

Nina felt ill, her stomach lurching as her breathing quickened, her eyes stinging all the while. The words flashed through her mind, endlessly repeating as she tried to retain some form of control. Her head pounded, sharp pains shooting through it as red lips and a mismatched gaze staring at her emerged from her ever shifting thoughts.

There was the laughter of a child, a small hand reaching for a doorknob. A warm voice called a dead woman's name. Spices and wood and the scent of lavender pervaded a hall with cream colored walls. A red smile flashed once more.

"I know who I am."

Nina let out a laugh. It was a broken thing, like the shattering of her mind, that turned to a sob carrying all the pain she'd bottled up inside of herself. All of the doubts that still haunted her mind had become too heavy a weight for her to keep carrying, and she crumbled beneath that burden, if only for that moment.

Her head was still pounding, the memories playing over and over too much of a strain. She wondered if that was how Fearnley would feel when he found out the truth and was glad she hadn't told him after all.

Maybe he'll never know, Nina thought. Maybe I'll just go mad.

That was what Nina felt was happening at that moment, her mind finally fracturing beyond repair. When she was finally able to gain some control over herself, her breaths calming even as her hands continued to shake, Nina felt exhausted—drained. More than that, there was a deep sense of hopelessness settling inside of her along with fear.

It was the fear that came from being uncertain of who she was, of who anyone in her life was. Nina couldn't trust her friends anymore, couldn't trust her own family if her memories could be so greatly altered. Most alarmingly, Nina knew that she couldn't trust herself anymore. Not when she wasn't sure that what she knew was the truth.

No, I'm not insane. I know who I am. And she knew that she was needed. Nina knew that there was a man in prison who had no one else to help him—to prove to the world that he was innocent. She knew that a woman had entrusted her with finding the truth before she'd died.

That was enough, at least for Nina. It would have to be enough.

She closed her eyes, took a deep breath, and willed herself to regain enough control to keep going. There was nothing else she could do now, but to keep going, to keep looking for the answers that would hopefully put the whole thing to rest. When Nina opened her eyes, a long breath escaping through slightly parted lips, she found that her hands weren't shaking as badly. Some of the determination she'd always held so close to her, the drive that made her who she was and the only thing that had kept her going through the harshest points of her life, returned in full force.

Nina stood, legs shaky and body still aching, but she stood and looked around the dreary motel room. The television was still on, something Nina hadn't noticed until then. A news anchor spoke with a serious tone and tired eyes about things that Nina couldn't find it in herself to care about in that moment.

Her notes, along with Fearnley's medical records, were still strewn across the small desk while the chair she'd been sitting on rested on it's side on the old carpet. Like it had the night before, Nina's laptop sat atop the desk, screen still displaying the smiling faces of those who worked at SEIN. Nina didn't dare look at it, not ready to face those mismatched eyes staring back at her. The revelation from earlier was still too fresh in her mind. More importantly, Nina wasn't going to allow herself to break down. Not again.

There were still things Nina wanted to do, and she would need to hold on to her sanity for a while longer for that. She rubbed at her eyes, which ached from both staring at pages upon pages of names and faces on a computer screen and the tears that Nina hadn't been able to hold back.

After a quick glance up at the clock, and one longing look at the as of yet untouched bed, Nina decided that whatever little sleep she could get would do her good. She was tired, both physically and mentally. Nina doubted she would last much longer if she didn't get some rest. Besides, she didn't know what to do. Not when she was so uncertain of so many things.

Against Nina's best efforts, her thoughts travelled back to the smiling face of the woman she'd thought was her friend. Her head twinged in pain once more.

Because my memories of Nat aren't real, she realized, thinking back to her last conversation with Fearnley. He'd mentioned headaches when he thought back to the night of Alice's murder. Nina was now certain it was because Fearnley's fragmented mind was trying to push aside the lies to reveal the truth hidden behind them.

For a minute, Nina thought about righting the chair at her side and taking a seat in front of the desk once again. She considered looking through her notes and searching for any other clues pointing to fabricated memories. Nina wanted to search her own mind, purge it of anything that could be false at the same time that she looked for any more lies that could have been fed to Fearnley.

No, I need to rest, she told herself. It was something that those who'd mentored her during the earlier days of her career had made clear to her—to rest when she could. With that in mind, Nina dug through her bad for more pain medication, hoping that would be enough to quell the ache in her head.

She didn't bother to change as she finally climbed under the multi colored covers of the bed not much later. Nina didn't find it so hard to fall into a light sleep. The day had been long. The morning when she'd first heard her phone ring, Ben's voice sounding anxious, seemed like something from a lifetime ago.

The ticking of the clock on the wall was almost hypnotic, the small sound seeming louder in the stillness of the room. It echoed inside Nina's head as she tried to find some rest, fading into a distant thing as Nina's breathing evened out.

That sound persisted, turning into the clicking of shoes on hardwood floors. It was a steady and familiar rhythm, as were the cream colored walls and the soft music playing from some unknown source. The scents of wet earth and damp wood filled the hall, familiar smells that made Nina think of home. That made her think of safety as a sense of fondness that she couldn't quite determine the origins of, rose up inside of her.

Her steps continued, steady and sharp as she walked farther down the hall. A single frame waited near the end, growing ever closer, gleaming even in the soft lighting. Nina's gaze was fixed upon it as she walked ever closer.

Three steps away.

The hall began to spin, Nina's head twinged with pain as she lost her balance. The world turned upside down and a sense of foreboding swelled up like a wave inside of Nina. She glanced up, the hall twisting and the frame just within reach.

Two steps away.

Her steps faltered, and then the hall was gone as were the scents of wood and earth. Instead, they were replaced by the harsh stench of disinfectant and blindingly white lights along a pristine hall. Panic coiled around her heart as the realization of where it was that she stood hit her. Nina took one fearful step back and suddenly, she was falling. Darkness wrapped around her, the rush of air vivid enough that she nearly screamed. She shut her eyes, and then she was standing on solid ground.

Once more, there was the smell of earth and wood and soft notes ringing out around her. Nina let out a shaky breath, and slowly opened her eyes, expecting the warm light and cream colored walls that had once been so unsettling to her.

She opened her eyes, and had to fight back a scream.

A mirror framed in silver hung before Nina, gleaming and spotless. No green gaze was found in it. Instead, it was a pair of mismatched eyes that stared back, sharp and colder than Nina had ever thought they could be. Lips painted a vivid crimson tone stretched out into a mocking smile and Nina felt her heart shatter once again.

Nina awoke with a scream fighting it's way out even as she pushed it back. Her heart pounded in her chest, as fast as the beating of the rain as it pelted the world lying just outside the still dark motel room she was in. Her hands shook and a sharp pain stabbed through her head as she sat up, still feeling exhausted. The clock on the wall kept ticking on steadily. Nina closed her eyes and focused on the sound, doing her best to match her breathing to it, to steady the wild beating of her heart.

The weak light of dawn slipped into her room through the slim gap between the curtains. It was time for her to leave.

Nina packed what little belongings she had with her, not taking more than ten minutes to do so. Soon after, she found herself in her car, pulling out of the parking lot of the motel. Despite her having spent only a short time there, Nina felt like that was a place she would always carry with her. The things she'd found in that room were the kind that were impossible to forget.

The rain from the previous day persisted in the form of a light drizzle that fell from dreary skies and dotted the windshield of Nina's car. All the while, there was a chill hanging around that made Nina's fingers stiffen from the cold. It was a relief when the car became warm enough to make Nina feel more awake.

After all, the desolate road before her wasn't making that any easier. It was quiet, with Nina only passing other vehicles occasionally. A sense of isolation, one that Nina had been struggling against since the previous day, took a hold of her. Once more, she found her mind wandering to her friends, to her family—to those she thought she knew but could no longer be certain.

No, not everything is a lie. It can't be, Nina told herself, and surprised herself with how desperate the thought was. With how much she wanted to believe it.

She pressed her mind to find something, anything, that could prove her whole life wasn't a lie. A simple sign that when it was all over, Nina wouldn't find herself with no one to turn to. That all of the people in her life wouldn't slowly fade from it. Once again, Nina thought of Fearnley, only now she wished she'd also been left in the dark about what had been done to her.

But this is what I wanted, she thought. It's what I was looking for. The truth.

Nina didn't like thinking that way. She didn't like turning something she'd always valued so much into a thing to be feared. For a second, Nina wondered what Iris would think of her supposedly fearless friend shaking at the thought of what more she could learn. The thought passed quickly, only to be replaced by the terrifying idea that maybe Iris wouldn't care—that maybe she, like Nat, wasn't the person Nina thought she was.

The thought hurt. More so than Nina had expected after she'd done her best to resign herself to the thought that the people she knew could all be lies placed inside her mind.

But why? Nina asked herself. Was it to keep an eye on me? Nat works for SEIN, if memories of her were planted among my own then there was a reason for it, a good one. Could they have known that Alice implanted her memories inside my mind too?

It was possible, after all, Alice had treated Nina for some time and it was clear that they'd done something to Fearnley's mind too. If Alice knew something she wasn't supposed to, it made sense they would keep an eye on her. Nina didn't think it was hard to believe that they would also be watching Alice's patients so closely. She just hadn't considered them planting memories in her mind to place a spy near her.

The admission of what Nat truly was pained her, but Nina knew it was something she had to accept. It was a fact that sank slowly into her mind, the memories she once thought were her own stirring as the image she'd had of her supposed friend faded and was replaced with cold, mismatched eyes and a mocking smile that had once seemed warm.

Nina shivered, despite the warmth inside the car. She turned on the radio, attempting to find a way to keep herself from dwelling in thoughts that would only muddle things up. If anything, Nina needed a clear mind, with everything going on around her at that moment.

"... expect some more storming near ..."

"... backed up due to a crash ..."

Nina switched through all the morning news and updates. She tried to tell herself it had nothing to do with her newfound fear of hearing her own name being mentioned.

The cops only wanted to question me. Ben said so, she reminded herself, knowing all too well that what she was accused of would lead to more than just a simple bit of questioning.

It was why she had run.

Nina settled on a station playing some catchy pop song, one that was in about a hundred commercials, but Nina still didn't know the lyrics to. It was good enough to distract her and chase away the lonely feeling that came with driving down such a quiet road for so long.

The sound of rain beating against the windshield was a constant, even as the songs changed and the early morning crept closer towards the afternoon. It was nearly noon when Nina stopped at a gas station. Her stomach was painfully empty and her car was in a similar state. Two other cars were parked off to the side while a large truck filled up.

Nina felt surprisingly glad to see other people, like a reminder that she wasn't alone in the world. She supposed that was what happened when loneliness and paranoia mixed together.

Nina walked into the gas station and headed straight towards the coffee, buying the largest cup available along with some packaged bread and a couple granola bars. She figured that would hold her up until she found her way to a town where she could get a hot meal. As she walked to the register, she passed a couple of prepaid phones, the kind she hadn't seen anyone use in a good while. Idly, Nina wondered how long they'd been there, hanging off a rack at an old gas station.

For a second, Nina stared at the blister packs of prepaid phones, hesitating for a moment before picking one up. She ignored the odd stare the woman at the register gave her when she picked up the phone as Nina paid. It probably wasn't often that someone bought one of the things, judging by the amount of dust that had gathered onto it, turning the clear plastic opaque. Nina was just glad she didn't say anything, just took her money and handed her back a short, half faded receipt along with a few coins. She could still feel the woman's stare as she walked out of the stuffy shop, the cold wind feeling like an improvement.

Nina headed to her car, her shoes clacking in a quick beat as she walked. The rain had stopped for a while, a few weak rays of sunshine streaming through the dark clouds overhead. Even so, there was a sense of gloom that would not dispel throughout the day.

To keep her mind off of it, Nina dug through the paper bag containing her purchases. She pushed away the food and pulled out the plastic pack with the phone she'd bought. It was a black, bulky looking thing. Something from an era long past. For the first time, Nina wondered if the thing would even work, and realized she should have thought of that first.

Too late for that now, she told herself, already looking for something to open the pack with.

It was after a short struggle that Nina managed to pry open the pack and pull out the phone. Her fingers slid against flimsy feeling plastic and she second guessed the impulsive purchase.

It might come in handy. That was the only thing she could tell herself to justify it. Anything else might just remind her of how much she wanted to hear a familiar voice.

Deciding it was better to not dwell on those thoughts at the moment, Nina began charging the phone while she ate the bagged bread she'd bought. The scent of coffee had permeated every corner of the car, something that gave the small space a feel of home.

There was still half a cup of the warm drink left when she pulled out of the gas station. The rain had still failed to return and the streaks of sunlight painted bright spots onto the dark asphalt. As Nina stared out through the windshield, the road stretching out farther than she could see, she could almost convince herself that things would work out. That she would get through it all.

Chapter 19

Nina pulled her coat closer around herself as she stood on the side of the road with a cheap phone in her hand and uncertainty in her heart. A car drove past her, stirring up a cold breeze that almost felt like a slap. Above her, the sky had turned darker, making it feel much later than it actually was.

All of this barely caught Nina's attention as she focused on the device in her hand, the plastic feeling warmer after being held for so long. Even so, she couldn't make up her mind.

I shouldn't call anyone, she told herself, trying to reason her way to an answer. It's too late to involve anyone.

Nina was well aware of that. She knew just how risky it was, especially after the people at SEIN had realized she'd taken Fearnley's medical records. She would be surprised if they hadn't already questioned her friends—her family.

Her father came to mind. Her father, who lived alone because she couldn't bear to live in a house filled with memories of her mother.

Nina felt her mouth go dry, felt a pain in her heart as she wondered what he would think if he knew of the mess she'd gotten herself into.

"Sometimes, you have to do what's right, even if it's difficult. And it usually is!" Her father had laughed when he told her that, and Nina had smiled along with him. That was before she'd known just how right he was.

He would understand.

The thought, along with the memory of his voice, were enough to get Nina to dial a familiar number. She held her breath as the phone rang, each sound seeming to stretch for far too long and the pause between them like a void. After what seemed like an eternity, someone on the other end of the line picked up.

"Hello?" the word was spoken with some caution that Nina was sure came from having a call from an unknown number. Still, it was good to hear her father's voice.

"Dad, it's me," Nina said, struggling to keep her tone even.

"Nina? Why do you have a different number?"

That was enough to tell Nina that her dad knew nothing of what was going on. Later, she would wonder what had made the authorities keep her father in the dark—or maybe it had been SEIN who'd wanted it that way. Whatever the case, Nina was just happy to be able to hear a familiar voice.

"Yeah, I lost my phone," she said with a forced laugh, hoping he wouldn't notice. "I guess I've just been distracted with work. Kind of lost track of where I left the damned thing."

"Sounds like you needed more time off," her dad said. Nina wasn't surprised. He'd always stressed how she should take care, not overwork herself. She smiled a bit at the thought, the first time she'd done so in what felt like an eternity.

"I'm fine, dad. Just as tired as usual," she lied. "How are you doing?"

"Oh, so now you're checking up on me?"

"Well, someone has to." Nina felt lighter as she spoke to her dad, some of the exhaustion that had persisted for so long fading away with each word her dad spoke. She heard her dad chuckle a bit and nearly laughed herself.

"I'm alright. You know hardly anything changes around here."

"You can't blame me for asking," Nina said. She thought of her hometown, of the quiet streets and the familiar faces that only grew older as time passed, hardly changing as if the place were frozen in time. She supposed that applied to her dad as well. He was still there, in that home he'd made for his family, with the same knick knacks lining the mantel and photos framed on the wall. Nothing had change, and for once, Nina was glad for that much.

Even so, there was something on her mind, something that maybe only her father could answer. Doubts that she needed to lay to rest. It was, perhaps, the main reason she'd made the call.

"Hey, dad, do you remember the girl I used to play with all the time? I used to go to her house sometimes." Nina tried to be vague, knowing it was the only way she'd get the answer she needed. Even if it wasn't the one she wanted.

There was a short pause during which her father must have been thinking over the question. Nina supposed it was a strange thing to ask. Especially when it had been so long since they'd last spoken. Nina felt a sharp pang of regret at all the time she'd wasted, all the calls she wished she'd made.

I'll make it right, Nina thought. Once this is all over, I'll make it all better.

"Can't say I remember much about your little friends back then," Nina's father admitted, drawing her back out of her thoughts. "I was always working, honey," he went on with some regret.

Nina wasn't surprised. He was right, after all. She could recall long days in which she'd wait for her dad to get home, her mother's reassurance that he was on his was the only thing that kept her spirits up. Nina could still picture the tired smile her father would give her as he walked through the door, and the way she'd rattle on about her day while they headed to the dinner table.

"Well, now that I think about it, I do remember seeing you with one of your friends a couple of times," her father said, a thoughtful tone to his voice as he clearly did his best to remember what the child had looked like. Nina listened with bated breath, thinking of Nat's dark hair and mismatched eyes. "It was a short little girl, reddest hair I've ever seen." Her father chuckled, and Nina felt like her heart was breaking all over again.

"Why do you ask? You thinking about home?" he sounded hopeful to Nina, something that only made the regret she felt stronger. She still worked up a laugh that she hoped was convincing enough. Nina hoped the brittle sound would be enough to fool her own father.

"Who knows, the holidays are coming. I guess I'm due for a visit soon," she said, knowing her father would like that. More than that, the idea of going home after everything was over was more appealing than Nina had ever thought it would be. She needed a familiar place where she could rest without worrying. A place where she could be with people she loved and be sure of who she was—that she belonged. "I just ran into someone who reminded me of her, is all."

"Ah, now it makes sense. I was starting to think you were getting sentimental," her father joked. They both knew all too well that Nina had always kept much of what she felt to herself.

"I don't think you have to worry about that any time soon."

"Well, I don't know honey. You are getting on in years."

Nina actually snorted at that. It was a dumb joke, the kind her dad had made for as long as she could remember. Still, she couldn't stop the laugh that bubbled out of her on it's own, true and bright. It was something she hadn't thought she was still capable of. On the other end of the line, her dad laughed along, and the joy in his voice warmed Nina's heart.

"How are you doing?" her dad asked once the laughter had subsided. "Are you back at work?"

"Yeah," Nina lied. She didn't stop to think about how much easier that had gotten. "I've been back for a bit. It's nice, gives me something to do."

"As long as you're not working yourself to death."

"I'm not, I promise. I haven't been doing much, no big stories or anything. It's hardly a step up from laying around, resting all the time."

"It's what's best for you," her father said. Nina could have laughed again. Only this time, there would be no joy in it, just a bitter amusement at wishing she could do just what her father suggested.

"Don't worry, dad. I'm fine," Nina said, managing to sound normal. Then, a thought crossed her mind. A fleeting image of her mother along with doubts that still dwelled within her. Nina hesitated for a moment, wondering if she should bother asking. Afraid of what answers she would receive.

"Hey, dad, do you remember ever just think of mom?" The words were out of her mouth before she could stop them. Nina held her breath, heart beating in her chest as her mother's face swam in her head. Her smile, warm and comforting, was something too important for her to lose.

The moment of silence between the question and her father's answer felt like an eternity. Slowly, time trickled by, and her father finally spoke.

"I think about her all the time, honey," her father said, voice soft and full of the love he'd always had for Nina's mother. "Just this morning, I started humming one of her favorite songs while I was making some coffee. Guess that habit of hers must have stuck onto me," he said with a chuckle.

Nina laughed, relieved, and felt her eyes sting and then overflow. The tight grip of fear on her heart eased and Nina felt like she could breathe again. Her mother, humming as she made dinner, a smile on her face when she heard Nina start to hum along with her from her seat at the kitchen table—that was a memory Nina held dear to her heart. It was a memory that she could now be sure was true.

"Why do you ask?" her dad said, curious.

"Just wondering. I've been thinking about her. Maybe it's just because of the holidays approaching, I don't know," she said, wiping her eyes with a cold and shaking hand.

"Well, she did always love the holidays."

"Yeah, she did," Nina said with a smile. "Hey, dad, I have to go now. I have some work to do and I'll be making a short trip for an interview."

"I thought you said you were taking it easy," Nina's father said, suspicion and amusement clear in his voice.

"I am, I won't be gone long. It's just a short drive away."

"Well, it's not like I can stop you." Nina could hear her father sigh, clearly exasperated. "You're coming over for Thanksgiving, aren't you?"

"Of course dad." Nina hoped everything would be over by then.

She thought of what it would be like to sit with her dad for a nice dinner. To know that she was safe, that things were okay. That Fearnley was free and Alice could finally find some peace. It seemed like a faraway dream, and a part of Nina thought of it as an impossibility. Still, it was a nice thought to indulge in, if only for a moment.

"Alright, I'll see you then. And don't forget to call every once in a while."

"I won't. Bye dad."

For a while, Nina stood there, staring at the now silent device in her hand and already missing the sound of a familiar voice in her ear. She wondered when she'd hear that voice again—or if she ever would in the first place.

A cold breeze swept by, making the wet streaks on her cheeks almost hurt from the chilled feel that hit them. She pocketed the phone, wiped at her eyes and walked back to her car, feeling just the slightest bit more light than she had before she'd dialed her father's number. A weight had been lifted off of her, the knowledge that her whole life wasn't a lie enough of a comfort to keep her going.

The road didn't seem as daunting anymore, not when Nina felt a little better about the things she needed to do—about the things she would likely find on her journey. More than that, it made Nina more certain of where she should go.

Alice had been scared, had known more than she should have. She needed comfort, a place of safety and the warmth of the people who knew her best. Alice headed home, to the family much like Nina had sought out her father's voice and the reassurance that came from reminiscing about her mother.

Her mind called forth the image of her mother, smiling as she stood next to Nina—of where the picture had once taken up a small space on Nina's wall. And then she was thinking of woods and the scent of damp wood and earth. The scents of home.

Nina thought of a small hand reaching for a doorknob at the end of the hall. Of the sound of footsteps on a hardwood floor, bouncing off of cream colored walls, and the warm voice of a woman. More than anything, she thought of Alice. She thought of the plea in her green eyes as she stared back at Nina from within a mirror framed in silver.

And then, there was a painting. Leaves of gold and red and bark the color of wet earth, the winding waters of a river and a bridge stretching over it. The woods beckoned to her, Nina's gaze far away for a moment. In the next, she was herself, and she wondered when the woods had called to Alice. When she'd first yearned for home.

Nina didn't know, not yet, but she would find out.

Chapter 20

The way to Alice's hometown felt like a long one. Nina thought it was most likely due to the anticipation that she felt . After all, she didn't know what she would find there. She just hoped there would be answers.

It was well into the afternoon by the time Nina reached the small town. At any other time, Nina would have described it as a quaint little place, with a feel that made her think of another era. The place was quiet, with Nina only spotting a couple of people out and about. She wasn't surprised by it, after all, the weather was less than favorable. It was bitterly cold as the sun sank ever lower and the winds became like shards of ice.

Small shops lined the streets, decorated with multi-colored lights despite Thanksgiving not having even passed yet. It made the town seem bright, cheery even. It all made Nina think of the picturesque little towns shown on holiday cards. The same sense of nostalgia those gave Nina were stirred up as she drove through the bright street.

She wondered if Alice had felt the same way when she went back. More than anything, Nina wondered if Alice had known it would be her last time seeing those bright shops and picture perfect streets.

The thought cast a shadow across the town, it tinged Nina's view of it with an air of sadness that she struggled to push away.

Not long after, she found herself driving away from the main street and past rows of houses with perfectly kept lawns. Decorations shone brightly, glittering like stars. A memory from a time when Nina was still a child flashed in her mind.

She could almost feel the cool glass of the car's window as she'd pressed her face close and stared at the brightly decorated houses. Nina had been vaguely aware of her parents smiling in the front of the car, her mother pointing out different decorations and Nina's outward joy at the sights obscuring the whisper of envy she felt at knowing all her family could afford was a small tree and a couple strands of garland.

That had been a very long time ago, when things had been easier. When her mother was still alive and Nina couldn't even begin to imagine what awaited her.

Those were the thoughts that were still swimming around in her mind as she parked across the street from the house where Alice had grown up. Nina pulled out the slip of paper where she'd jotted down the address, making sure she was in the right place. Once she was certain, Nina stepped out of the car and into the frigid afternoon, the sun sinking lower in the sky behind the dark clouds that painted the day a darker shade.

Nina crossed the street, and paused on the sidewalk, in front of a house painted a sunny yellow tone. The immaculate lawn was split by a walkway leading up to the entrance—a white door with a golden doorknob. Nina stood there and stared at the only thing that stood between her and the answers that she needed.

She took a deep breath, the cold wind feeling like shards of glass that pierced down to her very bones, and then exhaled in a mist that dispersed in an instant. With a sense of determination that Nina had sincerely missed, she began the walk up to the door, her steps loud against the concrete. They seemed to echo around the quiet street and Nina was almost tossed back into memories of a hallway and the steady sound of her own steps against hardwood floors.

Nina fought back against those thoughts, pushing them as far back as she could.

Not now, she told herself harshly. But in her heart, she felt fear. A fear of what awaited inside and what memories she might find herself trapped in. What would she see in her mind's eye as she walked into a place so familiar to Alice?

All too soon, Nina stood before that white door. She raised a shaking hand, ready to knock on the door and face Alice's parents. And then, she stopped.

Nina wondered what Alice's parents were doing at that moment. How were they preparing to face the first holiday season they would spend without their daughter? More than anything, she stood there and asked herself whether what she was doing was the right thing. If what doubts she had were reason enough to remind a grieving couple of the daughter they had lost just a short time ago—to pry open a wound that was likely still bleeding.

It's what Alice wanted, Nina told herself. She wanted the truth, she wanted me to find out what she knew. To find out who was after her. Alice wanted justice, and Nina would be damned if she didn't give her that much.

With a new resolve, she knocked on the door, a sharp sound that broke through the quiet of the night. A minute passed, and Nina began to wonder if maybe there wasn't anyone home. If maybe Alice's parents hadn't left town. If they hadn't run from a home that likely held more painful memories than they could handle, much like Nina had done after her mother's death.

Before she could reconsider, before she could hurry back to her car and pretend never to have been there, Nina heard the sound of footsteps. Someone was approaching, their steps growing louder with each second. A chill settled inside of Nina, her chest feeling tight as anxiety gripped her heart. And then, the door was opening, light pouring out through the slim opening and onto the dark street outside.

For a second, Nina thought of a small, pale hand wrapping around a doorknob. She thought of the scent of spring flowers and the laughter of a child as a door opened and a bright light poured out into a painfully familiar hall.

"Can I help you?"

Nina snapped out of her daze, and found herself staring at an older woman with a questioning look on her lined face. She clutched her sweater, a bright blue color, closer to her to stave off the chill that hit her as she stood in the open doorway. What really caught Nina's attention, though, was the woman's gaze.

Green eyes stared back at her, questioning and cautious. Nina did all she could to keep her mind from traveling back to a place in which she didn't want to find herself trapped once again. Not at that moment. With all the willpower she could muster up, NIna dragged herself away from that hall and the mirror hanging from it—from the near identical green gaze she'd meet there. She focused on the moment at hand, on the woman standing before her, waiting for an answer.

"Yes, good afternoon, I'm Nina Sheppard from the Daily Inquirer," Nina began.

"You're a reporter," the woman said, looking both cautious and disappointed at the same time. Nina wasn't surprised at the reaction. If anything, she was just glad to not get a door slammed in her face. "Are you here to ask about Alice? We've already given a statement."

Nina tried not to think about the way the woman's voice faltered as she spoke her daughter's name. More than anything, she tried not to let the brief flash of guilt she felt at that grow into something bigger.

"I am, I'm writing a story about who she was. About her work," Nina hurriedly said, hoping she could convince the woman to hear her out before she found herself speaking to a closed door. "I was hoping you could tell me about her."

The woman at the door—Alice's mother, Nina reminded herself—hesitated, hand still on the door, and Nina had to try very hard to give her time to come up with an answer. As aware as Nina was that she was running out of time, she knew she couldn't press the issue. At last, the woman seemed to come up with a decision.

"That's all you want to talk about? Just her work?" she asked, staring at Nina's face as if trying to find any hint of a lie.

"Yes, that's all. You don't have to answer any questions you're uncomfortable with."

Alice's mother gazed into Nina's eyes for a moment longer while Nina did her best not to look away from those green eyes. Finally, the older woman gave a slight nod.

"I guess I can try to answer some of your questions." Nina held back a relieved sigh at that.

"Thank you, Mrs. Cassill. I promise I won't take long."

The woman gave a weak smile and opened the door wider, stepping aside to let Nina in. As soon as Nina entered the house, she felt a welcoming warmth wrap around her. In that same instant, a familiar scent of jasmine wafted over to her. There was a twinge of pain in her head, gone in an instant along with the flashing image of a very familiar hall. She didn't dwell on that, just accepted that she would be fighting the memories struggling to burst forth for as long as she was in that home.

Alice—her memories, still vivid in Nina's mind—were fighting to surface as if being called home.

"Why don't we talk in the living room?"

Nina's focus was turned back to the woman in front of her, still clutching her sweater close to her body as if fighting off a chill that wouldn't leave. Her eyes, hauntingly similar to those of her daughter, were still fixed onto Nina. They remained on the young journalist's form for a moment longer before looking away and leading the way to the living room.

"I'm sorry for the mess, we're getting ready to visit some family. With everything that's happened, my husband thinks it would be better to get a change of scenery," Mrs. Cassill said. Nina recognized her tone as that of someone resigned, but disbelieving. Clearly, the older woman didn't think a change of scenery would make her feel better about her daughter being murdered. Nina couldn't say she blamed her.

"It's fine, please don't worry about it," Nina said, her head feeling somewhat foggy thanks to the scent of jasmine so thick it felt stifling and the memories still fighting to emerge. All the while, the soft sound of a piano could just barely be heard from somewhere nearby. It was nearly enough to send Nina's mind spiraling back into that now familiar foreign memory.

She was glad when she was finally able to take a seat on the couch, her legs feeling weak and the world starting to turn. Nina settled on the firm couch, took a deep breath, and felt the world right itself for just a while longer.

"Would you like something to drink?" Mrs. Cassill asked.

For the first time, Nina realised just how dry her mouth felt. Perhaps it was the nerves, or maybe it was just being inside of a place so familiar despite her never having been there. The house, and Alice's memories, were playing tricks on Nina's mind.

"Just a glass of water, please," Nina said, working up a small smile that felt stiff on her face.

Mrs. Cassill walked away, and Nina was left to take in the room around her. It was a spacious place, with warm lighting and a variety of knick knacks laying about. The mantel held framed pictures, the light bouncing off the spotless glass and silver frames glinting as Nina's gaze swept over them.

It was only a second that Nina looked at them, yet that was enough to have images flashing in her mind. There were woods in the fall, painted in warm tones. A bridge stretching across a winding river. A pale face staring back with pleading green eyes.

Nina didn't realise when she'd stood from her seat. Nor did she notice at what point she'd taken the handful of steps that led her to the mantel. All she knew was that she was standing there, a picture in her hand and a prickly feeling just building up in her eyes as she gazed at the photo in the frame she held.

It was Alice.

Or rather, it was the young girl that would someday become the woman in Nina's memories. She was bright. That was the first thing that came to Nina's mind. A smile, small but still filled with warmth, stretched across her face while her eyes seemed to shine. That single instant, frozen in a simple image, reminded Nina of just how alive Alice had been. It reminded her of why she was there in the first place.

"She was still in high school in that picture."

Nina was startled by the soft voice of Alice's mother. Somehow, she managed to keep a grip on the picture, her heart beating rapidly as she placed it back on the mantel and turned to look at the older woman.

"I'm sorry," she said, and wasn't certain what it was that she was apologizing for.

"It's okay," Mrs. Cassill said with a small smile. It was full of fondness as she looked at the picture Nina had just returned to its original place. "You know, it was hard to look at them for a while. My husband kept saying we should just take them down, at least until we came to term with things. I just couldn't bear to do that."

"I understand," Nina said, and only hesitated for a moment before continuing. "My mother, she passed away some years ago. It was hard for a while, just thinking about her. Being in the same house where she'd lived."

There was no pity or sympathy in Mrs. Cassill's eyes, just understanding as Nina spoke. It made it easier for her to talk about her own loss, knowing that the older woman felt much the same way as Nina had when the wound left by her mother's passing was still fresh.

"I'm sorry for your loss," Mrs. Cassill said, taking a seat on an armchair. Nina walked back to her own seat, a glass of water waiting for her on the coffee table. "Does it ever get better?" the woman asked after a moment in a quiet voice.

Nina thought about that, thought about the nearly unbearable pain she'd felt when her mother had just passed away. She remembered the way grief would tighten its grip on her heart with any stray thought of her mother that crossed her mind. And then, she thought back to the picture that had hung on her wall not long ago and the way she'd walked past it so often before Alice's memories made that too difficult a task.

"In time," she finally said. "The pain is always there, even years later. But there's also all of the good memories you have. Thinking about the people you've lost turns more into remembering and celebrating their life and less about mourning."

At least, that was what it had started to feel like to Nina. It was the way she'd think about her mother humming as she did housework or walked alongside Nina. Or the way her mother's laughter sounded. The scent of her perfume, a soft, floral aroma that made Nina feel at ease.

"I'm sorry, you're supposed to be the one asking me the questions," Mrs. Cassill said. Nina pretended not to notice the way she wiped at her eyes, instead turning her attention to her water and taking a sip from it.

"It's fine," Nina said, a small smile on her face. One that she was surprised to find was genuine. Mrs. Cassill smiled back—a shaky twist of her lips—before taking a drink from a cup of what Nina thought was tea.

"Now, you said you wanted to know about Alice's work?"

"Yes, I was interested in the project she was working on. From what I understand it had to do with neuroprosthetics. Hippocampal implants, I believe they were called?" Nina said, taking out her notebook and a pen from her bag. She flipped to an empty page while Mrs. Cassill thought over her question.

"She didn't talk much about her work the last time she was here," the woman said, tone quieting at the last part. "But I'm sure that wasn't the last thing she worked on. It was a recent project of her's. She was so excited about it." Mrs. Cassill smiled as she thought back to that while Nina's hand stilled as she'd begun taking notes. She looked up at the older woman, doing her best to hide her surprise.

"Oh, and did she mention what her last project was?" Nina asked. For a second, everything stilled, Nina's whole focus fixed onto the woman sitting across from her.

"She mentioned it," Mrs. Cassill said, apparently having failed to notice Nina's reaction. "It was something about implanting memories," she said, and Nina felt like the world was turning upside down all over again.

Chapter 21

The world seemed to quiet while Nina tried to process what she'd just heard. Words swam through her mind, echoing over and over again.

Nina stared at it for what felt like an eternity, and then she knew where she needed to go.

Implanting memories, Nina thought, and felt her mouth go dry. She'd known Alice's memories had been implanted in her head, but Nina had suspected it had been through someone else's doing. Or more like, she'd hoped that had been the case. More than anything, Nina had hoped that it had been someone else who was responsible for nearly driving her mad.

But she was afraid Fearnley's memories had been tampered with while she was gone. It made sense. Nina had expected for her patient to be different upon her return. Alice had been relieved when that wasn't the case. Someone else implanted memories into Fearnley.

Nina thought of the daughter the man thought he had and knew Alice couldn't have done that. Just like she couldn't have been the one to place memories of a childhood friend Nina had never known inside of Nina's mind.

Mrs. Cassill was looking at Nina with a curious expression. There was concern there, and Nina knew she needed to snap out of it and get on with her questions.

"Memory implants, that's interesting. I've read about them, seems like they're set to be used to treat psychological issues. Once the FDA approves them, of course." Nina remembered that, and she also remembered Ben commenting on protests against the use of implanted memories in therapy. By the way Mrs. Cassill shifted in her seat, she knew about the opposition to the idea as well.

"Yes, that's what they're meant to be used for, but to be honest," she paused, hesitating as she stared down at the cup in her hands. "Well, Alice wasn't very fond of the idea."

"Did she have other uses in mind?" Mrs. Cassil shook her head.

"No, she just didn't like the idea of tampering with others' memories. Alice—her work—was all about restoring people's minds, their memories. It's why she was so interested in hippocampal implants. As far as implanting false memories, well, I don't think she was comfortable with the idea, to be honest."

"Is that what she said during her visit?" Nina asked, her own mind whirring at the new information.

"She didn't, but she wasn't here for long. And there was this sense I got while she was here, like she was nervous about something." The woman frowned, her eyes taking on a look as if she were stuck in her own memories. Thoughts of her daughter and what might have been on her mind the last time they spoke. "I tried to ask her what was bothering her, but she would just say she was tired. Work had been keeping her busy. I didn't pry after that. Now I think I should have. Maybe then. . ." she trailed off, and Nina could see the pain the woman must have felt at that moment.

"Well, what's done is done," she said, with a finality that told Nina she didn't want to think about what could have happened if she'd intervened. The possibility that her daughter's death lay—in part—on her shoulders was too heavy a burden for her to carry at the moment. Nina wished she could have told her it wasn't her fault. That Alice had known something was wrong all along.

"If Alice wasn't fond of the idea of implanting memories, then do you know why she ended up taking on the project?" Nina asked, deciding it would be best to change the subject. Already Mrs. Cassill's hands were beginning to shake with the effort of keeping her emotions in check.

"I'm not really sure. Like I said, she didn't talk much about that particular project while she was here, and before that she'd been working on neuroprosthetics. It might have been because of her experience working with memories, but I'm not sure. To be honest, she might just have been pressured into it."

"Is that something that happened often?" Mrs. Cassill shook her head at the question.

"Not as far as I know, but Alice was always good at what she did. From what I've found out about the project, they wanted the best for the job. That was Alice." The woman was smiling, a sad little twist of the lips that was charged with pride and what could only be love for her daughter.

"Do you know for how long Alice worked on implanting memories?" Mrs. Cassill shook her head, something Nina had expected.

"No, but it couldn't have been that long. She called me a couple of weeks before she visited. It had been a while since we talked, since she was busy with work. That day, she told me about her work with prosthetics. I think she had a new patient. She said something about him making good progress. Alice sounded excited, but she usually did when she was working on something that she thought was interesting, or with people she truly wanted to help," Mrs. Cassill said, her eyes lighting up just the slightest bit at the thought. "I think, what Alice loved more than anything, was helping people. She liked helping them put their life back together."

Nina could have laughed at that, bitter and filled with a dark sort of amusement. She thought of Fearnley, sitting in a cell and the guilt that ate at him as he thought of Alice's death. Of her fractured mind, the cracks deepening with every passing day and the memories that haunted her refusing to disperse. And then, she thought of Nat. Nina thought of a mismatched gaze that turned to a green one even as her mind hurriedly shut away those memories.

But then, she looked up at Mrs. Cassill—at Alice's mother—who was still sitting in front of her. Her shoulders were hunched, her eyes holding a sorrow Nina knew all too well. She was, in that moment, just a vulnerable woman. A grieving mother. Nina didn't have the heart to tell her of the way her daughter had driven her to the edge of madness.

Instead, Nina asked another question.

"Do you think she came here to get away from work? Maybe take break from it all, if she was unhappy with what she was doing?"

Mrs. Cassill seemed to think about it, her eyes flickering to one side, a faraway look in them for only a moment before she turned back to Nina.

"Maybe she did. We thought that she might just have wanted to see how we were doing. Alice didn't visit often, so I suppose we were just happy to have her here. We didn't ask her about why she was visiting. She told us she couldn't stay for long, that she had work to do." The woman paused, hesitating before continuing. "She was here for a couple of days and slept for a good part of the first day. We thought she was just tired. It's a long trip and Alice made it on her own without any stops. The next day she was gone on a walk for most of the morning. We spent the rest of the time here, Alice didn't want to go out and we were happy to just have a chance to talk to her."

"Did she still look anxious when she left?" Mrs. Cassill nodded.

"She did, but maybe not as much as when she'd arrived. It felt like she was tired," Mrs. Cassill paused for a moment, the cup in her hand shaking slightly until Nina feared she would lose her grip on the delicate porcelain. "Sometimes, I wonder if maybe she knew something. If maybe she knew that someone wanted to hurt her." Her voice wavered, emotions she'd held back starting to overflow.

"Do you really think that's the case?" Nina asked, brow furrowed.

"I don't know anymore," the older woman said with a sigh, setting her cup down onto the coffee table. "They say it was a patient of hers. Someone she'd helped. I can't think of why they would want to hurt Alice, or why she would be afraid of her own patient."

She looked up at Nina then, her eyes shining with tears that she was fighting viciously against.

"Do you think anyone else would have wanted to hurt her?" It was a question Nina didn't want to ask, but knew that she had to. The older woman seemed to think about it, remaining silent for a moment before slowly shaking her head.

"To be honest, I don't know why anyone would have hurt her. It's still hard to believe it was someone she treated." She looked at Nina then, a questioning gaze in her green eyes. It was as if she was aware that Nina knew more than she was telling her.

"It's what the police say. As far as I'm aware, the man they've caught confessed," Nina said with a sigh, deciding it would be best to feign ignorance. After all, she doubted Mrs. Cassill would believe her. Nina was still having trouble believing everything she'd been through. After observing Nina for a while longer, as if trying to find a lie in her words, Mrs. Cassill let out a soft sigh.

"You mentioned Alice went on a walk while she was here, do you know if she might have talked to anyone else? Or where she went?"

"No, I don't think she really talked to anyone. She was quiet, always had a thoughtful look, like something was constantly on her mind. I don't think she even noticed anyone while she was out." She pulled her sweater closer to herself, crossing her arms across her chest. Nina knew she had to be done soon before Mrs. Cassill became too uncomfortable. "She might have gone to the woods. Alice always liked going there ever since she was little. My husband always liked hiking and used to take her along," she said with a little smile.

Her eyes took on a distant look that told Nina she was lost in memories of a happier time. After a moment, she seemed to come back to herself, her gaze focusing back onto Nina as she turned her eyes towards the younger woman.

"I don't know what made Alice come here, or why she took on a project she disagreed with. All I know is that there was something bothering her, and now she's gone." Mrs. Cassill's voice cracked at the last part, and Nina could almost feel the pain of loss—something that had once been so strong that Nina doubted it would ever go away.

For an instant, there was a flash of an image in her mind. There was the giggling of a child and a warm voice calling out. There was a woman at the end of a hall and a feeling of comfort that came with her presence.

Mom. The thought crossed Nina's mind before she could stop it and then there wa a stinging sensation building up in the back of her eyes.

Then, she was back in the cozy living room of Alice's home, a barely touched glass of water in front of her and the questioning gaze of a grieving woman boring into her. Nina forced herself to relax, willed her hand to stop shaking.

"I'm sure you'll get the answers you need, Mrs. Cassill," Nina said, not knowing what else she could say. More than anything, she knew there was nothing that would ever wipe away the pain the woman felt. "But I think Alice came here because she needed you. She needed a place that felt safe—comforting. You gave her that. Whatever it was that was bothering her, I'm sure she was happy while she was here."

Mrs. Cassill gave Nina a shaky smile, eyes glistening and lips pressed tightly. She didn't say anything, perhaps because the only thing that would come out of her would be a sob that, like a dam holding back a flood, would release the grief she had been holding back. Nina understood that much, and she knew there were no more questions she could ask.

"Thank you for your time, Mrs. Cassill. I know this wasn't easy for you, so thank you for listening and answering my questions," Nina said, and then made to stand. Her legs felt stiff—her whole body did—but she knew it was time to go.

"I'm glad you came," the older woman said. "Talking about Alice, it made me remember. You know, I think all this time I've been avoiding that. It hurt too much. Still does if I'm being honest." She let out a laugh that was weighed down by a deep sadness.

Nina smiled, feeling genuine relief at hearing that she hadn't cause the woman too much trouble. Perhaps it was because she offered her true understanding, because they both knew the feeling of losing someone who claimed such a large piece of their lives. When Nina looked at Alice's mother, she felt even more certain that what she was doing was the right thing, that it would all be worth it in the end. That they all deserved—more than the truth—justice, whatever form that came in.

For that, Nina needed one more thing before she could leave.

The water was cold as it splashed down onto Nina. She managed to catch the glass before it could roll off the table and hit the ground, shattering into a myriad pieces. The way she jumped at the sudden and frigid sensation on her legs was genuine enough, even if she fully meant to tip the glass over as she reached for it.

"I'm so sorry," she said, setting the glass down onto the coffee table. Water still dripped over the edge of the table and onto the floor, pooling at Nina's feet. "I'll clean it up."

"No, no, it's okay. Don't worry about it, it's only a bit of water," Mrs. Cassill said. "I'll clean this, why don't you go dry off? The bathroom is upstairs, first door on the left."

She gave Nina a quick smile and sent her off before heading to get something to dry up the mess. Nina tried not to feel bad as she walked out of the room and towards the stairs.

The house was nearly silent as Nina walked farther and farther away from where Alice's mother was. All of the sounds of her shuffling about in the living room were all but gone. Only the sounds of soft music drifted by as Nina climbed the stairs. Idly, Nina thought of how familiar the melody was.

Once she reached the top of the stairs, Nina felt a sense of apprehension, for the first time fearing what it was that she would find there. The very air felt tense, almost as heavy as the last couple of steps Nina had to take. She breathed in deeply, exhaled slowly, and stepped onto the second floor.

As soon as Nina's gaze landed upon a hauntingly familiar hall, she felt the world spin around her. A dreamlike fog settled upon her as reality blurred with the surreal memories that filled her mind. All at once, recalled the heavy scents of wood and earth. The petrichor smell that pervaded the air after rain and the spices that made her think of fall and trees laden with leaves painted in warm tones.

Then, there was the aroma of wildflowers, gentle yet vivid and warm like a spring day. There was the giggling of a child and the soft piano notes in the distance—the clacking of feet against a hardwood floor, the rapid beating of her heart, the call of a name by a loving voice. And then, there was the glimmer of a silver mirror at the end, a door opening with light streaming through, a small, pale hand—piercing green eyes that made Nina's heart clench.

All of these inhabited the same space for an instant that felt like an eternity, Nina's mind filled to the brim with all of those memories that had never been hers.

She stood there, eyes glazed over and nearly swaying on her feet as she stared straight ahead. The hall seemed to stretch out for miles, and the first step that Nina took felt like too great an effort. Even so, her feet moved on a steady pace as the memories continued to flood into her mind.

Cream colored walls seemed to close in around her as she continued to move forward and a mirror that she wasn't sure was there glittered beneath the warm light. Nina could hear blood pounding in her ears, nearly drowning out the soft music that still played. In the back of her mind, there was a strong feeling of wrongness struggling to make it to the surface, like a warning going ignored. Nina walked on.

She was just a few steps away from gazing into the mirror, wondering what she would find there. And for once, the thought of green eyes staring back wasn't so unsettling.

It's not a memory, Nina told herself. This is real. This is where Alice lived.

Nina stopped, closed her eyes, and then pushed away those memories for the time being. Her head was pounding, enough so that she wondered if she would make it further down, if she wouldn't simply collapse from the pain and the memories overlapping with what lay in front of her very eyes.

She could see the hall, stretching out in front of her, and a closed door at the end, the contents behind it unknown. A child's laughter echoed in her mind.

"Alice." A now familiar voice followed soon after and Nina had to fight not to turn around.

Almost there, she thought instead, mere steps away from the end of the hall.

She ignored the frame on the wall, her eyes focused straight ahead even as green eyes flashed in her mind. Nina forced herself not to dwell on that, not to think about the ever changing pictures and the pleading look from a dead woman. Finally, she stood in front of the door, and her hand reached out towards it—scars just peeking out from the edge of her coat, so different from the small pale hand of her memories.

Nina's fingers closed around the doorknob, cold metal that snapped her out of those memories. For a moment, she simply stood there, wondering if she truly wanted to see what was on the other side of the door. It took her only a second longer to make up her mind.

The doorknob turned beneath her grasp and, with a soft push, the door opened to reveal the room inside. Instantly, Nina knew where she was. The room was painted a soft yellow tone making it seem brighter than the rest of the house. It was well kept, with the shelves free of dust. The bed, covered in a duvet with a simple floral pattern, was perfectly made. Nina had the thought that the room was welcoming and warm—the two things that Alice had needed the most when she'd decided to return to her childhood home.

At that moment, as Nina stood on the doorway to what was unmistakably Alice's room, she yearned for her own home. A place that she had left long ago, when the memories had been too much and the pain of loss too fresh in her heart. It made Nina wonder how Alice's parent's could keep the room as if their daughter could return at any moment instead of locking the door and shutting away those memories of her.

Nina stood there for a second longer before turning and softly shutting the door. Her hand slipped from the doorknob as she rested her forehead against the door and let out a tired sigh.

"What am I doing?" she said in a soft voice, and wasn't certain of what it was that she was questioning. All Nina knew in that instant was that there was a grieving woman downstairs and she'd just intruded into the last reminder of her daughter.

With that, Nina turned to leave. She took only a couple of steps before she stopped and turned to the frame that still haunted her mind. Nina looked at the picture in a black frame, light bouncing off the spotless glass, and couldn't help but stare.

There, on the wall, was one of the paintings that had so often crossed her mind. The warm tones coloring the leaves stood in stark contrast to the dark bark of the trees and the grey sky just barely visible through the foliage. It was an image that was well known to Nina, one that was like a brand to her mind, searing itself onto it until she could recall every line and spot of color.

Chapter 22

Saying goodbye to Mrs. Cassill had been difficult, perhaps because Nina knew there was so much she wasn't telling the woman. Things Nina knew Alice's mother would want to know.

She'll know soon enough, she thought to herself, and it wasn't as comforting a thing as Nina had hoped.

The things Alice had done, most likely even the things she had known, were things that would cast her in a different light. Things a mother would be pained to learn. Staring into green eyes, so like Alice's, set on a face lined with grief made Nina question once again the value of truth. Whether it was truly so worth the pain it would bring about to the people who learned of it.

It's what Alice wanted. And so it was, as far as Nina knew. Alice had wanted it so desperately she'd shattered Nina's mind—against all she had dedicated her life to.

With a smile that felt too brittle to keep up for very long and tremors running through her hands from the emotions she was holding back, Nina bid the older woman goodbye. She heard the door close behind her as she made her way down the path in the front yard and saw the last slivers of warm light fade as she was shut away from a place that felt so painfully like home. The warmth of her own mother a memory that seemed achingly fresh after the short visit.

Suddenly, Nina felt glad that Alice's father hadn't been home at the time. It would have been too much for her to handle, especially given her recent conversation with her own father. The promise she had made, one she was uncertain if she would be able to keep, clinging to the back of her mind.

With that, Nina made her way to her car through the chill that could not be beaten back by the last remaining rays of sunlight that managed to break through the dark clouds overhead. The warmth of the car did nothing to make her feel any better. Nina was still too preoccupied with all that she'd talked about with Mrs. Cassill, but more than that, she was surprised at how much she felt like she knew Alice.

Not much time had passed since the memories began to swim through Nina's mint, leading her to the woman who'd put them there. To someone who was long gone and Nina had never known. And yet, after all that had happened, all that Nina had done to get the answers that she needed, she'd learned more about Alice than she would have liked. Even if Nina was still picking up the pieces of who she used to be, trying to arrange them back into what she once was and hoping the cracks weren't so apparent.

As night fell over the town, and knowing that there was nothing she could do while it was so dark, Nina went in search of a place to spend the night. She didn't want to spend much longer in the time, didn't think she could risk staying in a single place for too long given the way she'd left, but she had no choice. Nina knew where she had to go, and she also knew that she wouldn't be able to find her way while it was dark, with a storm due to arrive so soon.

With that in mind, Nina found a small hotel—one of the few large chains she'd seen in the place—and got a room that was a definite improvement over the last place where she had stayed. The room was simple, with a bed that was perfectly made and lights that seemed too bright given Nina's aching head. She dropped her bag as soon as she walked in and glanced at the desk she was provided with. For a moment, she considered taking out the files that were hidden in her bag and going over them once ore, but she knew there was little more she would be able to find in them.

In the end, exhaustion—the same one she had been fighting against for days—won over, and Nina decided to simply take advantage of the warm room she had at the moment. After all, something told her she would need all the energy she could get for the day ahead.

That night, as Nina lay in bed, she was painfully aware of the near absolute silence that surrounded her. The sounds of the city—always awake, always in motion—were gone, taking the small comfort the sounds provided her. She lay there, memories she didn't want passing through her mind.

A young child's laughter rang through her mind. Nina closed her eyes, tried to shut away the memories as she did the same to the world around her. Still, the sound reverberated through her mind.

Alice, she thought, and pictured the young girl in the photo on Mrs. Cassill's mantel. She thought of green eyes staring through a mirror. Of the face of the woman the laughing child would become. A woman long dead.

"Alice," a warm voice called, and Nina felt her heart break as she thought of her own mother.

"We don't have a daughter," the words echoed in her mind.

A mocking smile on painted red lips stretched out across a pale face. Mismatched eyes stared at her—through her. Fearnley sat in a prison cell, thinking of a daughter he didn't have. Her mother hummed at her side.

Nina curled up on the bed, her hand going up to her head and the pain in her heart growing with every memory that she was forced to recall. Around her, the room remained silent, still. All the while, Nina fought against the onslaught of memories that refused to disperse. Eventually, the exhaustion that had plagued Nina became too strong.

Slowly, the room faded into darkness along with the memories, offering Nina a respite. For once, her mind was silent, and Nina only wished it could last longer.

All too soon, she found herself staring up at the white ceiling of her room. The still dark room was just as silent as when Nina had fallen asleep. For a moment, she was confused about where she was, about why she wasn't in her apartment. Then, the memories all came rushing back to her and she felt her head spin as she sat up.

The conversation with Ben and the trip she'd so unwillingly taken. Her roadside conversation with her father and the visit she'd payed to Alice's mother. The truth about just how much of her mind had been changed. It all came back to her, tossing Nina into a life that felt like it should belong to someone else.

Like a dream that she wanted to wake up from.

Unfortunately, Nina knew better. She knew there was no way out of the nightmare her life had become other than to keep moving forward. And so, Nina got out of bed, the room feeling cold as she got ready to leave. The first rays of the sun were just emerging from, streaking thin lines of gold and orange over the horizon.

It didn't take long for Nina to gather her things and make it out to the car, where she sat for a minute as the inside of the vehicle warmed. There was no one out at that time, it still being much too early for most people to even get out of bed. Nina knew she had to get an early start. After all, she couldn't be sure of what she would find that day.

She drove out of the town, a short distance that was almost eerily quiet. Nina saw only a handful of people on her way to the edge of town, all looking like they sorely wished to be back under the sheets, most gripping a cup of coffee like a lifeline. Nina briefly considered stopping by to get a cup of her own, but decided against it.

As picturesque as the town was, Nina didn't think it wise to linger. Already she had risked much by speaking to Alice's mother. There was always the chance that someone would ask questions and the answers would lead them to Nina. With SEIN and the police looking for her, Nina didn't think that would be a good thing.

Soon enough, Nina was driving along a road framed by trees with leaves of red, orange and gold that fluttered down to the ground with each breeze. Some distant part of her mind thought of the scenery as beautiful. It was peaceful, bright, almost warm against the chill of the late autumn morning. The first rays of sunlight filtered through the foliage reminding Nina of light hitting stained glass.

She couldn't help but regret that she was there under such unfortunate circumstances.

After a moment, Nina opened the window, the cold air stinging her face as it rushed into the car. It was still a pleasant feeling, refreshing as it seemed to sweep away the last vestiges of sleep that clung to her. Nina took a deep breath. The wind carried the scent of a coming storm—moss and ozone and wet earth mixing with dark wood. Something in the back of her mind, a niggling thought that grew ever more persistent, made Nina pause.

For a second, she could see the hall and hear a gentle melody drifting by. There was a frame with a picture that Nina could almost see. It was all gone before her mind could register what had just happened, before she could fully visualize the painting that rested in the frame.

Nina pulled over to the side of the road and sat there for a minute before stepping outside. The wind felt like a fresh breath and Nina enjoyed the feel of the cool breeze on her face. She closed her eyes, basking in the sensation for a moment before she took in the area around her. It was, much like the rest of the road she'd passed during the drive, silent and desolate with only the soft rustling of the trees as the wind swept past them and the distant call of a bird.

The day was brighter, the sun finally having emerged as the clouds parted for a short time, though there was still a haze that painted the world in dull tones. Nina took in the scenery, and was hit by the familiarity of it all.

A forest in the fall, she thought, recalling the paintings she'd seen so many times in both her dreams and waking moments. The memories that Alice had put in her head—the ones she'd purposely manufactured to tell Nina something—had so often revolved around a forest painted in warm colors.

Wet earth and damp wood. The scents permeated the air all around her. And lavender. She thought of Alice's home. Of the tranquil melody.

A pale hand pointed at a point on the painting, and Nina could see what could only be a bridge stretching across the river winding through the forest.

With those thoughts and images still running through her mind, Nina went back inside the car. She pulled up the cheap phone she'd picked up at the gas station and searched for a map of the surrounding area, the one she'd saved earlier in case she lost herself in the unfamiliar roads.

The town was still near enough that Nina could find where she was quickly enough. She could see the winding road, a dark line that cut through the forest. Landmarks dotted the portion of the map taken up by the surrounding woods and it didn't take her long to find the nearest river. It wasn't far, and Nina didn't hesitate to make up her mind about heading there.

As she drove, she thought about Alice—thought about her hiking in those same woods with her father. Nina thought about what memories Alice might have formed there. How important they must have been for her to seek comfort and safety there.

And then, Nina wondered what it was that she would find there.

Alice had traveled all that way, had left a patient to someone else's care. There had to be a good reason for that. Nina only hoped she was following the right trail.

She finally reached the place where a hiking trail began and parked on the side of the road stepping back out onto the cold. Nina glanced around, making sure there was no one around, and lamented the lack of a better place to leave her car. After all, she didn't want to draw attention to herself. Resigned to having to leave her vehicle out in the open, she grabbed her bag and made her way over to the treeline, the narrow dirt path seeming to call to her.

Nina paused for only a second before taking a step forward. The scents of wet earth and damp wood seemed ever stronger as she was swallowed by the forest around her. Dried leaves were crushed beneath her boots with a sound that felt too loud for the silent forest. Nina's eyes took in her surroundings as she carefully made her way along the path.

Despite it being clear enough to walk on, there were still fallen branches and underbrush she had to be wary of. Nina couldn't imagine many people using the path during that season. The cold would keep most people away and the constant rain they had endured turned much of the dirt to mud, digging holes into the path that were deep enough to be dangerous for anyone who wasn't paying attention.

At that moment, Nina wished she had more experience with forests. She'd never been much of an outdoors person, having lived in the city for most of her life. The only times she'd ever been in any place even remotely similar, was when she went out on school trips. Even those were only hazy memories to Nina, having taken place so long ago.

A child's laughter rang in her mind. Nina did her best to silence it even as as she couldn't help but think of the grieving woman she'd spoken to the previous day. A woman still mourning her child.

Nina shook her head to rid herself of the thoughts, but even then there were more flowing into her mind.

The scents of jasmine and spice filled the air as her steps clacked against hardwood floors. Ever changing paintings hung on the wall. A pair of green eyes stared from a mirror, pleading even as the face they were set on remained impassive. Mismatched eyes and a red smile seemed to mock her.

Nina stumbled, her foot twisting painfully as she stepped on a leaf covered branch. Her bag swung violently, making it all the harder for her to regain her balance, and she met the ground a moment later. Her gloved hands took most of the impact, and she was on her knees before she knew it.

Quick breaths left her as she stared down at the ground. The only sounds that could be heard were the sounds of her breathing and the soft rustling of leaves in the wind. Nina could still feel her heart pounding in her chest as she wondered if she would ever be free of the memories invading her mind.

That's why I'm here, she thought, a desperate plea to herself to keep going. Just get up, you have to get up.

Ignoring the new aches and pains she'd gained from her fall, Nina stood. She took a moment to brush herself off before picking her bag back up.

You're almost there. Then you'll know what Alice wants from you.

The thought reminded her of why she was there, helped her regain some of the resolve that had steadily been slipping away from the moment she awoke. She was still cold and tired—more so than she had ever been in her life—but she had to keep going. Not for Alice, not for Fearnley, not for anyone other than herself and the fractured mess of a mind she'd been left with.

Nina was in a search for the truth that Alice might have died for. That much would always be true. But, along the way, it had turned into more than that. Much was riding on Nina figuring out what was going on. There was Fearnley's freedom, justice for Alice's family, and the peace and relief that would come from knowing that she wasn't just going insane. That the memories still invading her head were there. That she wasn't simply broken beyond repair.

For all of that, Nina stood and took a step forward. Her hands stung, her knees ached and a dull throbbing had started up in her head, but Nina kept moving. Eyes forward and mind set on finding what Alice was leading her to, Nina continued down the dirt path.

She continued even as it began to drizzle, the drops so small Nina barely felt them touch her skin. Still, there was the chill that set in as she continued on her way with little to protect her from the turn in weather. Nina was almost relieved when she finally reached a bridge all too like the one in the painting of Alice's memories.

It was made of dark wood, nearly black thanks to the constant drizzle. Nina was glad to note that it was in good condition. As she got nearer, Nina could hear the roaring water from the river as it rushed along, crashing against stones. The water was high enough to nearly touch the bridge itself.

Nina only hesitated for a moment before stepping onto the bridge. Wood creaked beneath her feet and Nina gripped the railing tightly with both hands. She kept a firm hold on the railing all the way across.

She didn't pause for a second, not even when the image of that same bridge on a sunny autumn day flashed in her mind. There was the gentle trickling of water beneath the wood and a breeze that was crisp, fresh, and carried the scents of the forest with it. A pale hand slid along the railing before it was replaced by the gloved hand presently wrapped tightly around the very same railing.

Nina's feet still led her with a steady stride until she was at the other end of the bridge. The wet dirt of the path was enough to make Nina feel relieved as soon as she stepped onto it. Her mind cleared as she continued on her way down the path she'd been following, wondering when she would find what it was that Alice was leading her to. More than that, Nina was doing her best to keep her thoughts focused on the moment at hand, memories of a past that was not her own constantly threatening to surface.

It was stifling, to try to find her way inside her own head when everything was so muddled. When Nina felt like she was trapped in a crumbling building with no way out. When every other minute there was a flash of a crimson smile and green eyes staring through her.

That was probably why Nina almost missed it when a nearly overgrown path broke off from the one she was following.

It was a thin, winding patch of dirt that faded in parts under leaves and underbrush. Nina could see it heading uphill in a slight incline and hesitated as she considered which path to follow.

Alice knew these woods, she thought. She knew them, wanted to hide something here.

More importantly, Alice had led Nina there through the memories she'd implanted into Nina's head. Now, Nina had to trust that they had led her to the right place. With a deep breath, Nina turned to the new path and walked on, hoping she'd made the right choice.

Chapter 23

Drizzle began to soak through the jacket Nina was wearing and the wind had become even colder, the chill seeming to reach Nina's bones as she stared up at the small cabin the narrow path had led her to.

The cabin looked old, though well kept. A desolate air hung around it and the clearing it was situated in—still as if frozen in time. Nina couldn't help but stare for a moment, the small cabin seeming to stare back through dark windows. She stood there for what felt like hours before cautiously moving closer.

Still, nothing stirred as Nina reached the door, the inside of the small cabin remaining dark. Bracing herself, Nina reached out to grasp the doorknob and gave it a turn. She was almost surprised to have it open, but then she remembered that was what Alice wanted. That was why she was there in the first place.

There was a staleness in the air when Nina stepped inside. Dust mixed with the scents of wood and earth while shadows seemed to dance as light poured in through the doorway. Nina pulled out her phone, using it as a flashlight to look around the place.

It was sparsely furnished and consisted of a single room. Nina thought it had probably been used for hunting at some point. Most likely, it was a place that had been in Alice's family for a while. There were a couple of bunk beds on one end of the cabin, both bare though Nina could see some blankets folded and stacked on the top one. A small stove and a table with a set of chairs made up most of the other pieces of furniture. Nina looked through the cabinets in the room, all of them empty save for dust.

Nina stood there, the only light that which filtered through the windows and emanated from her phone, and found herself lost as to what she was supposed to find there. For a second, she wondered if there was even anything to be found. If the whole thing hadn't been some worthless hunt for something that was never there. Something her broken mind had conjured up.

No, there has to be something here, Nina thought. There was an undercurrent of desperation to that, one Nina didn't want to think about.

Before she knew what she was doing, she was searching the cabin. It was dark and cold, Nina's fingers feeling stiff and her body cold. The bag she'd carried was left on the floor as she searched every nook and cranny she could reach. Nina ignored it, all of it, and kept searching, only to come up empty handed.

Alice's eyes flashed in her mind.

Red lips smiled as mismatched eyes stared mockingly at her.

A mother's voice called for her child.

Nina sat back, her head aching and her heart pounding. A heavy feeling settled in the pit of her stomach as a rush of panic rose inside of her. The cold seemed to finally settle upon her as she found herself shaking. Outside, the rain began to fall in a steady, harsh beat while Nina sat still. Her mind was a rush of thoughts and memories, enough to almost make her want to scream.

Her hands shook, and Nina could almost feel the scars on her arms pulling at her skin. Even so, the ones in her mind were ever more apparent. They tugged at the frail remains of her own memories, shattering and scattering them until Nina wasn't sure what was left was ever hers.

Green eyes flashed in her mind's eye once more, and Nina felt a surge of anger that she'd been fighting against for a long time.

There was anger at Alice. Anger at the way she'd tampered with her mind to get what she wanted. At the way she'd broken a man now sitting in prison. Anger at the woman she'd seen as a childhood friend for lying to her about such a big part of her life. And there was anger at herself for allowing memories that weren't hers to drag her into such a mess.

At that moment, Nina found that she didn't much care for the truth. She didn't care about who it was who'd killed Alice or what it was that the woman had known. All Nina wanted was to go home. To see her father.

To be the person she'd once been instead of a shattered fragment of herself.

Nina sat on the floor of the cold cabin, and for the first time, she truly felt the loss of all that had been taken from her. For the first time, she truly considered giving up. Nina thought about the pieces of her old life she would be able to salvage and tried to convince herself it would be enough. That the memories haunting her would fade away with time.

She told herself all of this even as the idea of Fearnley languishing in prison surfaced. Alice's mother, grieving in a home filled with memories of her daughter. The people Nina had left behind and the questions she would have to answer when she returned. It all made her realize that there was no going back. There was only one option for her—to move forward.

Nina felt the anger—the loss and pain—drain out of her. Hands shaking and a dull throbbing still slowly fading from her head, she stood.

The cabin was just s dark, just as desolate, as it had been when Nina first walked in, but Nina gazed upon it in a different light. She saw it not as a worn cabin, but as one of the only places where peace and safety were a guarantee. It was a place where Alice knew no one would look.

And she did all she could so that I would find it.

The thought made Nina wonder just how Alice had known that Nina would make it so far. That she wouldn't simply give up or succumb to the madness that she felt lurking so close to her, waiting to wrap itself around her at any moment. Alice hadn't known her, hadn't know how far Nina would go to find the truth behind the memories in her head.

She didn't, Nina thought. But she had faith. She had hope.

And then she was killed. Nina felt the remnants of the anger she'd felt towards Alice leave her. Green eyes flashed in her mind, and Nina reached a hand up to her head.

"Why did you bring me here?" she asked, and wasn't certain why she did so in the first place. "What did you want me to find?"

Nina began to search the cabin once more, this time in a less frantic manner. She swept the walls with the light of her phone, sliding her hand along the wood. The rain continued to rage outside, a rush of sound that was almost deafening. Idly, Nina thought of how difficult the journey back would be if she didn't head back soon.

She thought of wandering the narrow path strewn with fallen branches and roots in the weak light of the waning sun, a storm raging around her, and knew she should get going before it was too late. Getting lost in the forest was not something Nina wanted to experience.

Her thoughts were cut short as she searched the area around the bunk beds, dust having gathered atop them. She looked up at the top bunk and caught a glimmer of light that lasted for a second. With a furrowed brow, Nina climbed up one of the steps to get a closer look and felt as if her heart had stopped as her gaze fell upon a picture hanging over the bed.

It was a small thing, the frame plain but the glass clear enough to reflect the light from Nina's phone. Nina paid little mind to these things as she focused on the picture the frame held.

A landscape painted in warm and earthy tones greeted her, the woods so similar to the ones she had just trekked through. Leaves were scattered on the ground at the foot of bark painted a dark brown. Above it all, hung a dark sky, streaks of weak light breaking through the clouds. Nina stared for what felt like hours before reaching out to pull the picture down.

Unlike everything else in the cabin, the frame wasn't nearly as dusty. There was a thin coating over the top that was easily wiped away. Nina noted how it lacked the distinctly aged look everything else had and could almost picture Alice placing it there during what would be her last visit—placing it there for Nina to find.

She climbed down, juggling her phone and the frame, before walking to the small table on one corner of the cabin. There, Nina carefully inspected the object, certain it was the exact same painting she'd seen so many times in Alice's memories. The ones she'd felt so relieved to realize were there in the place of a mirror and green eyes that seemed to stare through her.

Nina shook away those thoughts, and instead turned the frame around to open it. She felt her heart pounding in her chest, her hands trembling just the slightest bit as they turned the small latches holding the back in place. The seconds it took to pull away the back and reveal what was inside felt like hours until, finally, it was gone and Nina was able to look at the white expanse of paper broken by a small memory card taped to the back.

She felt her stomach sink at the sight of the small, innocuous object. It sat there, unmoving, while Nina stared, frozen without knowing what to do next. The simple action of stretching out a hand and taking the small card took too much of an effort.

Still, Nina soon had it in her grip, the tape peeling off with ease and the frame left on top of the table, open and forgotten. The small bit of plastic in Nina's hand felt ridiculously insignificant for something that could potentially be of so much importance.

Outside, the rain had lessened to a light shower. Nina decided it was time to leave. She walked away from the cabin moments later and didn't once look back.

Chapter 24

The hike back to the road where Nina had left her car was a long and difficult one, perhaps more so than when she'd first walked down the same dirt path. She felt the presence of the memory card Alice had left like a heavy weight she had to carry. Thoughts of what the card could contain—of what questions it might answer—played incessantly through her mind.

Throughout the whole walk, Nina paid no mind to either the rain or the cold. She walked with a single minded purpose, doing her best to navigate through the underbrush, the fallen leaves having grown slippery due to the rain and mud. Nina still stumbled as she walked, nearly falling what must have been a half dozen times.

Finally, just as Nina was starting to fear she'd gotten lost, the dark asphalt of the road became visible. A glint of light upon silver told her that her car was just ahead as well. She let out a relieved sigh as she emerged from the woods, looking worse for wear but whole and lacking the hopelessness she'd fallen into on the way to the cabin.

The warmth of the car was a welcome sensation, wrapping around Nina the instant she stepped inside. She took a moment to just sit there, leaning back against her seat and letting out a long exhale, eyes closed and attempting to rid herself from some of the tenseness that had gripped her upon finding the card.

It's what I've been looking for, she told herself.

And yet, she found her hand hovering over the card. Unable, or perhaps, unwilling to see what it hid inside.

Just get it over with, she thought. Get it over with and go home. Go back to your old life.

Nina nearly laughed at the thought. She was all too aware of how unlikely it was that she would ever be able to go back to who she had once been. Things had changed—she had changed—and there was no going back. Not anymore.

Finally, she pulled out her laptop, something she was immensely glad to have grabbed before leaving. The memory card was like new, and Nina wasn't surprised when she was easily able to open it and see the files it held.

There were several files, each labeled and most likely perfectly organized. Nina didn't get a chance to look through them before her attention was taken by a single file.

From Alice.

The cursor hovered over the file for as long as Nina's gaze remained fixed upon it. There it was, what Nina had been looking for all along. Proof that it wasn't all in her mind—that she wasn't going insane.

Alice had been there. Had left something there. More importantly, she'd led Nina there, and now Nina just hoped the answer as to why that had been the case—why it had to be her—was contained in the small card Alice had hidden in the cabin. That thought was enough to make Nina open the file with a simple click.

She was surprised when there was a video there, she felt her heartbeat quicken at the thought of facing Alice again. Of seeing those green eyes staring back at her. Nina hesitated for only a second before deciding to view the video.

The screen was black for a moment, the sounds of slight rustling audible before the image of a very familiar face appeared. Alice, green eyes and alive, sat in front of the camera. She looked different, with her hair tied back and wearing casual clothing, though the same tired look was found in her eyes. Dark circles marred the skin beneath her eyes and the paleness in her face could not be healthy. She looked, Nina thought, sickly. Given the stress she must have been under at the time, Nina wasn't surprised.

It was still a striking thing to see.

"My name is Alice Cassill, I am a Neuroscientist working for the South East Institute of Neurology, otherwise known as SEIN. Currently, I am working on a project regarding implanting fabricated memories into patients. This research is meant to help those with traumas recover through the removal or replacement of negative memories."

Nina sat back and listened to Alice's voice—a soft, measured tone—the rain outside just picking up and the howling winds the only other sounds. She sat there and couldn't tear her gaze from the woman on the screen even as her heart clenched painfully and a mother's voice calling for her daughter echoed in her head.

"Despite all of the research that has been done, the procedure is still risky. Memories are a delicate thing and the misuse of this knowledge is something that, to some, outweigh the benefits. The ethics of implanted memories is still a controversial enough topic that receiving approval for further testing and development has been difficult."

Nina recalled the conversation she'd had with Ben in what seemed like a long time ago, when they'd sat inside a cafe and talked over coffee. Back when Nina had still thought there could be a simple solution to her crumbling mind. At that time, Ben had mentioned people protesting—opposing the very thing Alice was now talking about.

She thought about Alice's mother. About how certain she'd been that her daughter hated what it was that she was working on. Nina thought about how Alice had seemingly wanted to help people pick up the pieces and move on with their life, attempting to reconcile that image with the one of the woman who'd ultimately broken her mind.

The same woman who hesitated on the screen before continuing. There was something in her eyes, some desperate expression mixed with helplessness that looked wrong to Nina. Perhaps it was because, in the memories placed in her mind, Alice had always stared back impassively, but seeing such vulnerability was unnerving.

"I've decided to record this in the event that anything should happen to me," Alice paused, glanced down and then back up at the camera, resolve in her eyes. It was a moment in which she seemed to consider what she was doing and the cost of it, before finding it was worth everything. "The FDA will not authorize the use of this procedure and is intent in shutting down the experiments we are conducting. They think the ethics and risks aren't worth the payoff, but those in charge won't allow the FDA to shut them down. The recent attempt on the Commissioner's life was due to this."

Nina felt cold all of a sudden, a heavy weight settling in the pit of her stomach as she recalled the news of the Commissioner of the FDA passing away. It was something she'd paid little mind to. Now, she wished she'd looked further into it.

"We're being kept in the dark, we're being told that our work will help people, but it's a lie. What we're doing, it's being used to brainwash people, to lie to them about who they are."

Thoughts of Fearnley rushed to the front of Nina's mind. Of the man who'd thought he'd killed a woman he'd hardly known, who thought he had a daughter who'd never existed. And then, there was a crimson smile, and Nina felt a sharp pain shoot through her head.

"The man accused of killing the Commissioner was a patient. Though I wasn't the one to treat him, it's my belief that he is not, in fact guilty, and was instead framed. False memories were implanted in his mind to convince him of his guilt." Alice paused, her brow furrowed and lips pressed into a tight line as she seemed to think of what it was that she was saying. At the same time, Nina couldn't help but think of Fearnley.

Fearnley, who could recall a murder he hadn't committed, who could still hear the gun going off and the life leave his victim's eyes. Whose mind had been shattered beyond repair—who missed a daughter he'd never had. Fearnley, who sat in a prison cell, an innocent man paying for a crime used to hide the truth.

Nina felt sick at the thought. But she couldn't help but feel relief in knowing that she had been right. That Fearnley was innocent and that the evidence she'd uncovered might set a man free.

"The files from this patient—every visit, every treatment and even the fact that he ever came to us—had been erased. With the help on one of my colleagues—Dr. Marcus Han—I managed to save some of it along with other documents proving that what people are being told isn't what is really being done at SEIN. I don't know how much it will help, incomplete as all the records are, but at least it proves something is wrong. Something is going on, and I don't know how far those in charge will go to keep it all under wraps."

Alice let out a sigh, tired and resigned at the same time. She leaned back a bit, stared at the camera, and then Nina watched her expression fall just the slightest bit. There was something in the way she looked, something in her eyes, that made Nina's heart clench.

"We are being watched. The authorities can't help us, there's too great a risk to attempt handing this information to them. I don't know who to trust, I don't know if there's anyone who can be trusted.

So, I'm leaving this information in the safest place I can find, at east until I feel it is safe enough for the truth to be revealed."

Nina watched as Alice stopped to take a deep breath, eyes closing for a moment, and knew what it was that Alice was so resigned to. She knew. Nina thought, and the image of her empty office surfaced for an instant.

"To whoever finds this, if anything has happened to me, please know that I am sorry for what I've done. Time and circumstances have convinced me that the only way to keep this information safe is to hide its location only in my memory." Nina saw the guilt clearly in Alice's green eyes.

"I think, what Alice loved more than anything, was helping people." That was what Alice's mother had said, and now, Nina found that she truly believed that. Even with all that she'd done—to Nina, to Fearnley—Nina could look into Alice's eyes and see the knowledge of what she would have to do gnawing away at her conscience.

"If you find this, thank you. I trust that I've chosen someone who will do the right thing."

The video ended. Alice's face disappeared from the screen and Nina was left to stare blankly at the place where she had been. After a moment, Nina went back to the other files, her mind still working through the information she'd gotten from Alice's video even as she sorted through the records Alice had managed to retrieve. It was an attempt to answer at least some of the questions she'd been left with after watching Alice's video.

As she'd said, there were patient records, though incomplete. It was all information that had most likely been wiped away like fingerprints at a crime scene. Nina glanced thought them, wishing once more that she'd looked into the attack on the FDA's commissioner. Perhaps then she would have had a better idea of what it was that she should be looking for. She did, however, have one name she could search for.

"Marcus Han," Nina muttered, thinking of the man who'd apparently helped Alice. Nina pulled out her notes, flipping through the pages until she found the one where she'd jotted down the names of those involved in the same projects as Alice and wasn't surprised to find that Dr. Han's name was missing.

Nina nearly laughed at having briefly expected things to be easier.

Alice said they were erasing information, Nina thought as she closed up her laptop and set it aside.

"I don't know how far those in charge will go to keep it all under wraps." Nina felt a chill run down her spine as Alice's words came back to her. For the second time that day, she pictured Alice's empty office and then Fearnley sitting in a barren prison cell.

Against her will, Nina began to wonder if the worst hadn't happened to Dr. Han. If maybe, like Alice, he'd been silenced already.

No, I can't get bogged down with that kind of thought, Nina told herself, shaking herself and setting her notes aside. She looked at the card Alice had left for her to find and pulled it out, still in awe at how such a small thing could be so important. I need to make sure this gets to the right people.

Nina tucked the card away into one of her coat pockets before starting up the car. The sun was already sinking as she started down the road, the sky still a dull grey, and all Nina wanted was to keep driving until she was out of that town. Until she was back where she belonged.

But that life—the one where she knew what her place was, where she knew who she was—felt much too far away for her to get to at the moment. Nina felt the weight of the card in her pocket, a small thing that felt like too heavy a burden, and knew her time in that town hadn't yet come to an end.

Night was fast approaching, and Nina still had much to do.

Chapter 25

Nina sat at the small table of her hotel room, her notes and laptop in front of her and silence her only companion. The bright light from her screen made her eyes feel tired, and the call of sleep grew stronger with every passing second. Still, Nina found her mind stuck on a single thought, one that had occurred to her from the very start but had been pushed away by all else that had happened.

Why her?

Why, of all the people she had treated, had Alice chosen her? Nina hadn't known Alice, and yet something had told Alice that her memories would be safe with Nina. That Nina would find the truth—along with the card holding the final pieces of the puzzle.

And she was right, Nina thought, the notes in front of her suddenly looking like the obsessive writings of a woman near madness.

She thought of the things she'd done, of the lies she'd told and the people she'd hidden everything from. Of the home and the life she could never go back to.

Nina looked around at the dreary room she was sitting in, at the small bag that carried most of her belongings. She felt the tremors in her hand and the ache in her head that had become so common she could hardly remember a time when they weren't present. Above all, Nina felt the exhaustion that ran through her body even as she was determined to keep going. The very determination that, somehow, Alice had known would drive her to find the truth.

She knew, Nina thought.

Alice had treated her, had probably been there when Nina received the implant that had changed her life. More than that, Alice had seen Nina's file and knew what she did for a living. Alice knew that Nina was a journalist, had probably looked up her past work. If anyone would follow the trail Alice had left, it would be Nina.

By a twist of fate that neither could have ever imagined, both women had been connected, their lives and minds so deeply intertwined that Nina almost felt as if she knew Alice. Now, Nina was left to untangle the threads that tied her to the other woman. All the while, below the strong sense of determination mixed with a seemingly never ending exhaustion, there was the pain and anger Nina was starting to suspect would always be present when she thought of Alice.

More than that, there was now the knowledge that Alice hadn't been the only one to tamper with her mind.

Nina thought of a wide, mocking smile she'd once thought of as warm. She thought of mismatched eyes and red lips on pale skin. She thought of the friend she'd never had and the betrayal that was still like a fresh cut in her heart.

Someone had planted memories of a friendship she'd never had, all to keep an eye on her. To make sure that she didn't get close enough to the truth.

No, Nina though. No, it was to make sure that, if I did, they would be there to stop the truth from getting out.

The realization left her feeling cold. It made a chill run up her spine as she wondered how long they had been watching her and how much they could possibly know.

They never stopped me. They were counting on me leading them to the evidence Alice had gathered. She looked at the card laying next to her laptop and marveled at how far people had gone for it. To destroy a mind for such a small thing—it was nearly enough to pull a bitter laugh from Nina's lips.

She sighed, sitting back as she listened to the wind still raging outside. The thought that the same people who'd built up a lie to keep an eye on her could be in that town, watching her, wasn't nearly as alarming to Nina as it should be. Perhaps it was because of her profession, because of all of the things she'd seen and heard.

If they wanted to watch Nina, to see her fall apart as she chased down what they were trying so hard to hide, then they were welcome to. Nina was just going to keep goin. To keep searching for a way to get the evidence that Alice had given her life for out to the public.

She sat up straight, fingers flitting about the keyboard of her laptop as she searched for information on Dr. Han. Despite the sense of dread she felt when she thought of what might have become of the man who'd helped Alice, Nina still held onto the last shred of hope.

That hope was shattered moments later as she ran across the first of many articles detailing his death. Nina felt her shoulders slump as she drew away from the screen, eyes still staring at it as she leaned back. The smiling face of a dark haired man who could only be Marcus Han stared back at her. Beneath it, there was the picture of a wrecked car, the metal so badly bent and burned that Nina couldn't even tell what model or color the vehicle was.

All she could think of was the thick scent of smoke and the heat that seemed to grow in intensity with every second. The bitter taste of burning wreckage—suffocating even as she gasped for breath. The wailing sirens that seemed much too far away. Searing pain and heat. The tang of blood in her mouth.

Nina came back to herself after a moment that felt like an eternity, hands shaking and heart pounding in her chest. In that instant, she was all too aware of the scars she still carried. Of the memories seared into her mind, memories Nina didn't think would ever fade.

She exited the page, not needing—or wanting—to read any further. Already she was wondering if Dr. Han might have felt the heat of the flames as they grew around him as Nina had, or if he had been spared that pain. Nina felt her stomach turn. She closed her eyes, did all she could to push those images out of her mind, to focus on something—anything—else.

They killed him. The thought came to her suddenly, like a heavy weight dropping onto her shoulders. He knew too much, so they got rid of him. And then they did the same to Alice.

Nina struggled to understand how anything could be worth the lives of so many. How anything could be worth destroying so many minds.

She thought of the woman she'd considered a childhood friend and the memories that still flooded her mind at the slightest trigger. Of the way her mind was still slowly falling to pieces. Of the hall that was still there, waiting in the back of her mind even after it had served its purpose.

All of a sudden, Nina could recall the scent of lavender and spices. A woman called for her daughter. A child's laughter rang down the hall.

Nina closed her eyes, took a deep breath, and grounded herself. When she opened them, she was still staring at the bright screen of her laptop. The sound of the wind felt like a distant thing as Nina sat at the small table. The feeling of helplessness she felt at that moment—something Nina had struggled with as of late—threatened to overtake her.

Not now, she told herself. Nina sat up, looking through other articles. As much as she wanted to avoid reading about Dr. Han's death, Nina knew it was necessary.

She looked past the more gruesome details, at least for the time being. Instead, Nina focused on things like dates and locations. Some part of her wasn't surprised to find the man had died not far from the SEIN building. He'd been on his way home when he lost control of his car.

What caught Nina's attention was the date of Dr. Han's accident.

She pulled her notebook closer, turning the pages until she found what she was looking for. Nina read the date on the page and then looked back up at the article she'd been reading. Then, she thought of Alice, and the fear she must have felt as she recorded what would be the last video of her life. Alice, who would then return to work, and soon after have the one person she could trust to help her die in a seeming accident.

All at once, things made more sense to Nina.

Marcus Han died after extracting Alice's memories and Alice knew she was running out of time. And so she'd done the only thing she could do. She'd found someone she thought had the best chance to follow the clues in her memories.

She'd found Nina.

Alice had found Nina and thought she was the best chance she had. A day later, Alice was dead, and the only thing she'd left behind were the memories haunting Nina's mind.

Some of the bitter anger Nina had held close to her heart since learning of what Alice had done to her ebbed away. There was still hurt and anger there, lurking just behind all the other overwhelming emotions, waiting to break through to the surface and pour out of her. Now though, they were only a whisper of what they had once been, and Nina found that what she felt more than anything else in regards to Alice was sympathy.

She thought of the woman still mourning a daughter—a pain she could only imagine the depth of. Nina thought of the bright woman who'd been murdered because she knew too much. Because she wanted to do the right thing. And then, she thought of the sacrifice that had been made for the sake of that—Alice's morality having been cast aside as she broke an already fractured mind.

And I'm still here, Nina thought, and had to ask herself why. Because I'm still me. Because I still have my morals.

Nina had lost many things since the accident and the surgery that followed. She'd lost pieces of herself as time wore on, the fragments of who she'd been breaking off with every revelation, every painful truth she uncovered, until the parts that were left were unrecognisable. Now, Nina felt raw, vulnerable—but that core part of her, the part that held onto her belief in the value of truth and the determination that had carried her so far—remained unchanged.

As Nina sat there, undeniably changed, she knew she was where she should be.

With that thought, Nina inserted the card back into her laptop. Nina didn't know how much longer she had before either she was found or her mind gave out, but she would do all she could before either of those things happened.

Her eyes burned as she stared at her screen, going over the numerous files Alice had procured. There were petitions to the FDA to allow for further testing of implanting memories, patient files that had been wiped from SEIN's records, meticulously kept notes on the people Alice and her colleagues treated.

Nina read through them all, connecting the dots as her gaze remained steady on the screen. The silence around her was, for once, a welcome thing. Free of distractions—of things that could trigger some hidden memory, Nina kept a steady pace as she flipped through the documents. She couldn't help but marvel at how much Alice had been able to save.

When the quiet of the room was broken by a knock on the door, Nina couldn't help but jump. She was startled at both the sound and that anyone would be outside at that hour and in such bad weather.

For a while, Nina simply sat there, staring at the door, petrified at what—or who—could be on the other side of it. She could feel her heart setting a frantic rhythm, pure panic spreading through her body until she felt she could hardly breathe. The knocking came again, and Nina's body finally responded. Hurriedly, she grabbed her bag and shoved both her laptop and notebook into it. The card Alice had left was pocketed along with her keys while another round of harsh knocks sounded.

The curtains were drawn, the fabric thick enough that Nina couldn't make out so much as a silhouette. As quietly as possible, Nina moved over to the door. She looked through the door's peephole and felt panic clawing at her throat.

Mismatched eyes stared straight ahead, familiar even in the dark hall.

A name—one that might be just another lie—rose to Nina's throat and was drowned out by the dread that rushed through her. Nat, her mind supplied, despite Nina's best efforts to stay away from thoughts of the lies she'd been fed. At the very least, it served to help Nina snap out of her shocked state as she stepped back before turning to grab the sole bag she had with her and the phone that still rested on the desk.

A loud sound startled Nina and she watched in horror as the door swung open. The rain outside seemed deafening to Nina's ears and mismatched brown eyes seemed overly bright even in the dim lighting. Gloved fingers were wrapped around a handgun and Nina's hear was gripped with fear the sight.

"Hello, Nina." Crimson lips stretched across a pale face in a cold smile and Nina knew her time had run out.

Chapter 26

The wind felt cold as it swept through the open door and the rush of rain outside was like a roar in Nina's ears. Even so, she heard the quietly spoken greeting as she stood rooted to the spot. Her legs felt stiff, her body cold as her mind seemed to turn into a rush of thoughts and calls to run. And then, the gun glimmered in the light as the hand holding it shifted and Nina knew that wasn't an option anymore.

"What do you want?" she heard herself ask. It was an odd feeling, to feel so distant to all that was happening around her, as if she were only a spectator watching as the scene unfolded before her. Nat looked at her curiously, unsettling eyes sweeping over Nina.

"So you know about me," she stated. Clearly, she had expected for Nina to have found out the truth. Perhaps in the same way that Fearnley's implanted memories had degraded, the lies in Nina's mind had slowly been washed away, driving her suspicions.

There was a distinct lack of surprise on the woman's face, a nonchalance as she stood there with a gun in her hand that was frightening to Nina. Enough so that she wasn't certain as to what to do. All she was aware of was the woman blocking her way and the card Alice had left resting in her pocket—a weight that seemed too heavy at the moment.

"I did some reading," Nina said simply, her mouth dry and her hands trembling even as she tried to hide it. Fingers slid across the phone she was holding and she fought to remain calm as she spoke. "Why did you do it?" she found herself asking.

Nat—if that truly was her name—took on a curious, maybe even amused, look. Her brow rose and her lips curved just slightly.

"Why did I do what? You'll have to be more specific than that, I'm sure you have a lot of questions."

The mocking tone made something in Nina snap, even as questions rushed through her mind. Alice's empty office. Fearnley sitting in a prison cell. The life Nina had lost. There was no answer that would justify any of that.

"Why did you kill them?" Nina asked at last. She glanced at the open door and the gun in the other woman's hand before returning her gaze to those mismatched eyes. A sharp pain shot through her head. Nina ignored it. Focused on the moment.

"I didn't kill anyone," Nat began. "All I did was help clean things up. Wouldn't have been good for anyone to recall inconvenient details."

"So you framed people—patients. You made them think they'd done your dirty work." She watched as the woman in front of her shrugged.

"It was a sacrifice that had to be made."

"Because of what? Your experiments?"

"The research we're doing would have a greater impact than you know. The potential in memory implants—"

"Isn't worth the risks or ethics, is it? Alice thought so," Nina interrupted. She watched as annoyance overtook Nat's face.

"Alice didn't understand that sometimes risks and sacrifices are necessary for advancement. All of the things we'd learned would have been wasted if we'd let her do what she wanted with the information she stole. The FDA already didn't want to approve any more testing."

"So you had the commissioner killed."

"He wouldn't change his mind. We thought if someone else took charge, someone more pliable, things would be easier."

"You killed people," Nina said, her voice heavy with disbelief as all of the things she'd learned were confirmed. "You ruined lives, you broke into my mind." She stopped, something occurring to her and she felt a new wave of horror sweep through her.

"You broke Fearnley's mind." Fearnley, who had been drowning in guilt until he couldn't take it anymore and had to turn himself in. Nina thought of the man who's life had crumbled away around him—a sacrifice in a game that he never should have been a part of.

"His mind was already a mangled mess, just like yours," Nat said, apparently tired of the exchange. She raised the gun, stepping closer to Nina, the glint of the metal weapon like a warning. It took all of Nina's courage not to step back. "And now you can finally be at peace."

Nina swallowed, heart racing and blood pounding in her ears. The trembling in her hands worsening.

"And who will you blame for this?" she asked, voice as steady as she could manage. The barest hint of a tremor still hiding beneath each word. Nat smiled, crimson lips curving on her pale face.

"The hotel manager was fairly rude," she said.

The gun pointed straight at her. Nina could see into the dark depths of the barrel, could feel a chill run down her spine at the thought of what awaited her at the other end. The phone in her hand slipped from her fingers and fell to the ground with a clatter as Nina moved.

Thoughts of Ben flashed through her mind, of how he'd once suggested she learn self defense. Gratitude flowed through her as she reached for the gun. The maneuver came to her easily, adrenaline and muscle memory combining in that instant. Her grip on the other woman's arm was like steel as she twisted the weapon. It went off, the force of it something even Nina could feel run through her body.

A bullet hit the ceiling, fine grains of dust and plaster raining down from the point of impact. Nina kept her grip, twisting until the weapon fell to the ground and then Nina took her chance. She let go with one hand, swinging with as much strength as she could muster.

She felt her fist connect with the woman's cheek, a small burst of pain shooting through her arm from the force. Nina was glad to see her knocked back, stumbling over the chair Nina had been sitting on and falling to the ground, dazed. Quickly Nina grabbed the phone she'd dropped along with the fallen gun, stumbling over her own feet as she hurried to the open door.

The night was cold and rain pelted her, icy drops that felt like shards against her skin. She ran to her car, not looking back, fingers searching for the keys she'd stuffed into her pocket moments before her room had been broken into. She fumbled with the keys for a second, somehow managing not to drop them, and was soon climbing into her car. It started immediately, something Nina was grateful for.

Tires screeched as she drove out of the parking lot and onto the rain slicked road. Her heart was still pounding in her chest, the adrenaline seeping away and leaving her feeling exhausted and cold. As she drove away, Nina spared a glance back through the rear view mirror and could just barely make out the woman staggering out of her hotel room.

Fear shot through her even as she reminded herself that she was fine, that she'd gotten away. A glance at the passenger seat where she'd tossed the gun reminded her of how close a call it had been.

The gun glinted as she drove passed a streetlight and she thought of how menacing the sight had seemed just a minute ago. Nina thought of how the void that was the barrel of the weapon had felt like such a terrifying thing. Fear had clenched her heart in that moment, a fear Nina hadn't felt since the night that had changed her life, when she'd laid beneath the night sky surrounded by flames and twisted metal.

For a second, Nina could feel the heat against her skin and the smell the acrid smoke that threatened to suffocate her. She could hear the wailing of an ambulance and see the dark sky watching it all past the metal and fire. Then, she shook her head, and the memories were gone, leaving only a desolate road ahead of her.

In that moment of calm, one that Nina feared wouldn't last, she reached for her phone. It was battered, a corner of the screen cracked, but still functioning well enough for her to send a message to a familiar number.

As she pressed send, Nina thought about the people waiting for her, about Iris and Ben and her father. A desire to see them, to speak to them—to gain some form of comfort from simply having them there for her—rose within her and she knew she had to keep going. Nina knew she couldn't give up.

The road stretched on before her, desolate and dark, and Nina hoped what awaited her at the end was better than what she'd just left behind.

Chapter 27

Rain fell down in sheets, beating against the dark asphalt as Nina drove out of town. Her hands clenched the steering wheel like a lifeline. Nina felt drained, all that had been keeping her awake and functioning up until then starting to wear out.

At her side, the gun she'd taken from the woman who she'd once thought was a friend rested along with her phone. The latter buzzed as a new message was received. Nina was not the least bit startled by the sound, having expected it. She still ignored it, knowing all too well who it was from and knowing it was best not to answer. There was nothing else she could do anyway.

It would be a long drive home. Perhaps even longer with the added exhaustion of driving through points where she would normally rest. Nina didn't for a second doubt that she was still being pursued. She was still in very real danger, that much she was certain of, and Nina didn't think it would be smart to take any more risks.

The sooner she made it home, the better.

Nina wasn't sure for how long she'd driven, her eyelids heavy and the dull pain of exhaustion running through the whole of her body. The hand with which she'd punched the woman back in the dreary hotel room still stung at times and a steady pain took over her head.

A red grin flashed through her mind. Mismatched eyes turned to green ones and a small hand reached out towards a door. Nina shook her head, focusing her gaze on the road even as the images remained there, in the back of her mind and threatening to burst forth. Nina found that she was too tired to hold them back for much longer.

Just a bit more, she told herself, despite not being certain when everything would be over. When she would be able to rest.

Once again, her phone buzzed, and Nina considered simply tossing it out the window. After all, it wouldn't be of any use to her any longer. It was just as she was thinking this that a faint glimmer in her rear view mirror caught her attention. She looked up and, through the fog that was growing thicker with each minute, she could see what were obviously headlights.

Panic seized her heart before she could even be certain of who the driver of the vehicle behind her was. The empty road that had just a moment ago been a welcome thing suddenly felt dangerously isolated as the car behind her grew nearer. As her heartbeat quickened and her grip on the steering wheel tightened, Nina found herself glancing back to the gun on the seat next to her.

For one brief moment, Nina considered what it would be like to use to gun. To feel the weight of the cool metal instrument in her han and the force she'd just barely felt back in the hotel room when it was fired. Nina thought of how easy it would be and was frightened.

She turned away, fixing her eyes on the road and speeding up. It wasn't a great shift in speed, but enough for it to be noticeable. Enough for her to be able to tell if the car behind her was truly following her.

Nina glanced back up at the rear view mirror, and felt dread welling in the pit of her stomach as she watched the other vehicle speed up as well. The fog and rain made it impossible for Nina to be able to tell who it was that was driving the other car, but she had a good idea. Mismatched brown eyes flashed through her mind. A sharp pain shot through her head. Memories of a childhood that was never hers threatened to surface.

For a second, Nina felt a twinge of pain at the thought of losing a friend she'd never had.

Nina sped up, overly aware of how dangerous a move that was. The rain slicked road glistened in the light of her headlights and the roar of the wind and the storm around her seemed deafening. Her heart thundered in her ears while the weight of the card still in her pocket felt like the heaviest burden she would ever have to carry.

The headlights from the other car were almost blinding as Nina glanced back up at the rear view mirror. She could just make out a silhouette past the light and rain that blurred her vision. For an instant, Nina thought she could almost make out Nat sitting behind the wheel. Could almost feel her staring at her with a glint in those sharp eyes of hers.

For the second time, Nina sped up, the road becoming a blur she could hardly keep up with. Her mind whirred as she thought of where she could possibly go. Of whether there was any place where she might find some semblance of safety. As Nina stared at the road ahead of her, knowing there was still a considerable distance between her and the next town, the answer was all too clear.

Nina was painfully alone and afraid she wouldn't be able to hold on for much longer.

She drove as quickly as she dared, still mindful of how dangerous the road had become due to the weather. Behind her, the unfamiliar vehicle grew closer and closer while Nina tried not to glance back too often. Already, her hands were shaking, the dull pain in her head growing in intensity. All the while, the gun at her side called to her—promising safety, peace.

The same gun that, not so long ago, could have taken her life.

Nina turned her gaze away from the weapon. A second later, her phone went off yet again, and it was a difficult thing to not pick up. At that moment, what Nina wanted more than anything, was to hear a familiar voice. To hear a friend—a real one. What Nina wanted was what Alice had sought in her hometown, when she felt like there was no one she could trust, and everything to lose. Comfort.

The promise she'd made to her father rose to the front of her mind. She thought of him, waiting for her all alone in a house filled with memories. Nina felt her eyes begin to prickle as the rain continued to rage around her and the wind swept through the trees with a sound like a hundred hushed voices. All the while, headlights followed her path.

She rounded a corner, wheels sliding on the road in a way that had Nina's heart pounding. The car behind her was close enough that Nina feared they would crash into each other. Somehow, they both managed to clear the turn, only for Nina to feel the car behind her hit hers.

Panic shot through her as she struggled to keep control of the car. Somehow, she managed it, the screeching of tires cutting through the storm and her heart feeling like it would burst out of her chest. She glanced back, wide eyed, and could just make out Nat sitting behind the wheel. They were so close that Nina could almost see the rage on the other woman's face.

The car behind her sped up, attempting to bump against Nina's. Even then, Nina didn't dare speed up any more, memories of fire and pain like a warning in her head.

Just a bit more, Nina thought, hoping against hope that she would be able to make it someplace where she could get help. As unlikely as that was in the dead of night, Nina had to hold onto that last shred of hope to keep going. All the while, the card in her pocket was an all too prominent weight.

Then, she felt the jolt of her car being hit once again, this time with more force, and Nina feared that would be the end of her journey. As she coped with what was happening, struggling to stay on the road, Nina knew she had no more choices. With a deep breath, she reached over to the passenger seat.

Her fingers slipped around the cool metal of the gun. The weight of it gave Nina pause, but only for a second as she saw the headlights behind her growing brighter. She thought of the woman driving that car and memories of a childhood that had never been her own flashed in her mind. Memories that made a twinge of sympathy that she shouldn't have felt, shoot through her.

Nina thought of a smiling child walking at her side. She thought of shattered glass and blood and the wailing of sirens. Her heart clenched even as her mind told her it was all a lie—to pull the trigger.

She heard the rain and wind roaring all around her, water hitting her face as she opened the window, and ignored it all as she stuck out her hand. The sound of the gun going off cut through it all, almost deafening to Nina's ears. Tires screeched as a bullet hit the car. The shock of it had been enough to startle the driver into swerving violently. Nina was jolted forward as her car was hit in the process, the vehicle sliding on the rain slicked road.

Fear gripped her heart as she fought to regain control, even as she knew it was too late. The car skid along the road, turning violently while Nina frantically tried not to crash. She saw the other car swerving, heading straight through her, and felt her heart stop seconds before the impact.

A sound like a cry echoed through the empty road followed by the shattering of glass. Metal twisted and bent in every way and the world turned as Nina tried to understand what was happening. Pain burst from more places than she could identify as he was tossed around, the seatbelt pressing against her and shards of metal and glass flying around her. Nina thought she might have screamed, a sound that was lost in the rush of sound around her.

And then, there was stillness and pain and the cool drops of rain hitting her face. There was a burning pain on her side and wetness that she was certain was blood. More concerningly, Nina felt heat. It was just a faint warmth at first that grew in intensity, a familiar thing that sent Nina's heart into a frenzied state. A scream drowned in her throat, stifled by pain and fear, blood bubbling forth and spilling through cracked lips.

Terror could still not dispel the haze taking over Nina's mind. I couldn't keep her from slipping away no matter how much she fought to stay conscious.

Nina heard the wailing of sirens in the distance.

They're too far, some distant part of her mind thought, past the horror and the panic.

The heat grew and the small relief that was the rain began to taper off. Nina lay there, amidst the mess of twisted metal, and listened to the sound of the only hope she had left.

Too far.

The thought was lined with a hopelessness like she hadn't felt before. Nina suddenly thought of her father, waiting in a home filled with memories. The thought of the promise she wouldn't be able to keep was her last as she lost her grip on the world.

Chapter 28

S un poured into the stark white room from the window, the city spread out past the glass. Iris stared out of it, a paper cup of coffee in her hand, the warmth of it seeping through her skin and steam rising from it. She watched as life went on, people went about their business.

At her side, her friend and co-worker rested on a spotless, white bed. She looked to be at peace, Iris thought. She certainly hoped that was the case. After all, Nina had been through a lot. Iris thought of what Nina had faced in the time during which she should have been recovering, and had to wonder how she could have missed the distress her friend had been in.

She was always good at hiding things, Iris reminded herself. She sipped the coffee in her hand, the hot drink providing some comfort. As she stared at her friend, Iris couldn't help but feel a sense of relief in knowing that she was safe. Nina was home.

"The case against Christopher Fearnley has been dismissed. Fearnley, who confessed to the slaying of Dr. Alice Cassill, has been released as new evidence has surfaced and a new suspect has been apprehended. . . ."

Iris glanced up at the television screen on the wall of the hospital room. The news anchor faced ahead with an impassive look as she read from the teleprompter, most likely unaware of the impact of the news she was reading.

". . . Katie Forrister, daughter of the new suspect, was seen entering the courtroom . . . ."

Iris watched the young woman on the screen. She avoided looking at the cameras surrounding her, voices shouting out questions. Her head was bowed, blonde hair obscuring much of her expression. Iris had an idea of what her face might have looked like.

Experience had shown her many times over the sort of pain family endured in similar cases. It was the pain of watching someone you loved be accused of doing horrible things. The feeling of finding out that they weren't the person you thought they were. Iris watched as Katie Forrister climbed into a car and couldn't help but feel bad for her.

She let out a sigh, turning away from the television and glancing instead at the bouquet of flowers resting by the side of Nina's bed, flowers that had been left there not so long ago. They were a lovely arrangement, with bright colors that softened the appearance of the room. It broke through the blank walls and the sharp scent of antiseptic. Iris thought Nina would appreciate them when she woke up once again.

The memory of the man that had dropped them off floated to the forefront of her mind. He was not what Iris had expected—though she wasn't certain what that had been in the first place.

Christopher Fearnley was an average man, thin and soft spoken. He was normal in every way, but Iris could still see what remained of what he'd been through in the dark circles still visible under his eyes. She could see it in the paleness of his skin and the lines on his face. But Iris could see more than the remnants of his time in prison.

There was relief in him, hope, things that they both knew were there because of Nina. And then, there was a warmth in his eyes, and gratefulness that seemed unmeasurable when he gazed upon the woman who'd saved him.

"She should be waking up soon," Iris had told the man as he stood there, he gave her an awkward smile and nodded.

"That's good." He looked back at Nina. "She'll be alright then?"

"The doctor says so." At least, physically, she would be. It was still uncertain how much of a toll everything had taken on Nina's mind. She'd woken up briefly while her father sat at her side, a nurse told Iris, and then Nina had gone back to the rest she needed so badly. "You can stay, if you want." Iris could only guess that the man would have much to say to Nina—much to thank her for.

He shook his head, sticking his hands into his coat's pockets.

"Thank you, but I should get going. Let her rest now. She's earned that much."

He'd been there for only a short time after hearing of Nina's condition. Perhaps it was for the best. Nina didn't need more stress as she recovered, something Fearnley seemed to understand.

" . . . Arrests have been made. The evidence gathered by Dr. Cassill is said to incriminate various high ranking officials at SEIN. A press conference will be held . . . ."

Iris only half listened to the news, already aware of what they would be reporting on. After all, she was the one who'd handed over the evidence. The one Nina had trusted with something that nearly cost her everything.

Something others had already died for.

Iris recalled the picture of Alice Cassill she'd seen while writing an article on the woman. Back before she had any clue as to what Nina was dealing with—a thought that still made her heart clench with what could only be guilt.

I should have known. The thought crossed her mind despite knowing all too well that Nina hadn't wanted her—or anyone else—to know. I should have paid closer attention.

As she looked down at her currently sleeping friend, Iris could almost hear Nina telling her not to think that way. That it wasn't her fault. A small smile stretched across Iris' face at the thought. And then, it was wiped away as she asked herself whether it would really be that Nina—the one she knew so well—who would wake up again. If it wasn't possible for it to be a different woman who lay in bed.

Just as the thought crosses her mind, there was a soft knock on the door. It opened a moment later and Iris saw Ben walk in. He looked tired, as he had since Nina had gone missing. There were dark circles under his eyes and a slump to his shoulders that hadn't been there the last time Iris had seen him. She supposed the pressure of all that was going on at work and knowing that Nina was in the hospital became a heavy weight for him to bear. And still, some part on Iris' mind wondered how heavy a burden Nina had carried all this time.

Ben smiled at her as he walked in, a brittle curve of his lips that faltered as he caught sight of Nina.

"How's Mr. Sheppard doing?" Iris asked.

"Better, I suppose. It helps to know she'll wake up again," Ben said, eyes still fixed on Nina and the subtle rising and falling of her chest as she slept. "But he's exhausted. As much as he wants to be here, he needs some rest."

Iris nodded, knowing how true that was. Nina's father had spent as much time as possible by his daughter's side, but knowing that she would wake up again had allowed him some peace of mind.

"Thanks for taking him home," Iris said with a smile. Ben only shrugged.

"It's the least I could do." His gaze settled on the flowers at Nina's bedside, his eyebrows rising. "Nice flowers," he commented.

"A gift from Christopher Fearnley," Iris said, taking a drink from her coffee. Ben seemed surprised, a thoughtful look on his face. "He was happy to hear Nina will recover."

"Of course he was, he owes her his life," Ben said. "The man would have wasted away in prison if not for Nina."

"She'd be happy to know that she was able to help." Iris could just picture her friend hearing about Fearnley, about how she'd managed to get his freedom for him.

"And then she'd try to tell us how she barely did anything," Ben added, a small quirk of his lips showing how the thought amused him. Iris could just picture it herself.

". . . The South East Institute of Neurology has ceased operations as authorities continue their investigation. Protests continue outside of the SEIN building over the controversial memory experiments . . ."

Both Ben and Iris paused to listen to the news, watching images of the SEIN building, surrounded by people holding signs as police officers kept a close eye on the crowd. It was chaos, and it was the last thing that the higher ups at SEIN wanted. The very thing they'd killed Alice Cassill and Marcus Han for. Iris found her eyes sliding back towards Nina and the flowers at her bedside and felt a sense of satisfaction as she looked back to the scenes on the television screen.

"You know, I'm glad Nina trusted you with the evidence she found," Ben said, eyes still focused on the television.

Iris thought about that, about how—in her desperation—Nina had chosen to trust her. In spite of all that had happened, of all Nina had been through, she'd still thought of Iris as someone she could rely on.

She recalled the surge of panic she'd felt when she'd been woken up by a message from a friend who'd seemed to have gone missing. Iris had looked at the files she'd been sent, confusion flooding her mind.

The short message that was more of a plea from Nina still stuck in her head. And then, there had been the unsettling silence after that, during which Nina hadn't replied to any of Iris' calls or messages. The unknown number from which Nina had sent a voice recording of her arguing with a woman—one who'd later been identified as the other victim of the crash.

The fear in her friend's voice as she'd spoken with the woman was something Iris doubted she'd ever forget along with the shot that sounded just moments before the recording was cut off.

"Yeah, I'm glad too," Iris said, still in a daze, her mind filled with thoughts of all that might have gone wrong. They sat there for a while, Ben only leaving shortly to get some coffee for the both of them, Iris' first cup having been drained long ago.

"What happened to the other woman? The one involved in the crash," Iris asked as they both sat with their drinks.

"She didn't make it," Ben said, direct as always. "Didn't see the doctor's report, but from what I heard, she was gone by the time the paramedics made it to the scene. Would have made things more difficult if we didn't have so much evidence about both her and SEIN."

"Nina was never one to half ass an investigation," Iris said with a shrug.

Ben snorted at that, knowing Nina well enough to know how true that was. The brief second of levity was cut short by a sudden gasp followed by a series of coughs. Both turned to the bed, Iris nearly dropping the coffee she was holding as her eyes settled onto Nina, who was finally waking up.

There was a rush of movement in the room as Iris hurried to help her friend settle down while Ben raced to get nurse. Help arrived in moments, a doctor looking Nina over while her friends watched anxiously.

"I'll go call Nina's dad," Ben said, getting an absent minded nod from Iris.

Once Ben was gone, Iris just stood off to the side and watched the hospital staff do their best to calm her friend. Nina's eyes were wide, tinged with fear still visible through the haze of confusion. Her eyes moved from one face to the next, but it wasn't until she caught sight of Iris that a spark of recognition was ignited.

Iris gave her friend a smile, one that wasn't so difficult to muster up as the relief of seeing her awake washed over her. After that, it was easier for Nina to settle down. Iris still stayed out of the way as the doctor looked Nina over.

It was only when her phone notified her of a message that she took her gaze off Nina. The text she'd received was from Ben, just a short note telling Iris he'd gone to pick up Nina's dad. She sent back a quick reply, letting Ben know Nina had calmed down and was being looked at by the doctor.

"Iris?"

The soft, shaky voice drew Iris' attention. Nina was looking at her, still confused but seemingly glad to see her friend there. Iris stepped closer, a smile in place.

"Hey, you had us all worried for a while there," Iris said, taking a seat next to the bed.

"What happened?" Her voice was hoarse, as if she hadn't spoken for years—or as if she'd screamed for just as long.

Iris hesitated for a moment, not certain on what or how much to tell Nina. A part of her wanted to wait for Nina's father to arrive. Then, there was the part of her that thought it would be best to spare the man having to tell his daughter everything.

"You were in an accident," Iris started. She watched as Nina processed the words, a distant look in her eyes.

"I was driving home," she said, getting a nod from Iris. Nina's brow furrowed as she struggled to decipher how it was that she'd ended up in the hospital. "From work, I'd finished late."

Now it was Iris' brow that furrowed, confusion and a sense of dread growing inside of her as some part of her recognized what it was that Nina was talking about. "Do you remember what you'd been doing before leaving?" she asked.

Nina thought about it, her mind most likely still muddled from the meds and pain and the disorienting feeling of waking up after so long. Iris waited, eyes sharp and heartbeat quickening with every second that passed.

"I was just at the office. Don't remember why, but I was at the office," Nina said, looking tired. It was like the effort needed to hold simple conversation was too much for her. Iris might have been more concerned about that, if not for the way her stomach seemed to turn as a realization hit her.

What Nina was recalling was an accident that happened months earlier—the accident that had ended with her getting a hippocampal implant. The one that had started the whole chain of events that led to Nina laying in the bed in from of Iris.

The realization was enough to make Iris' head spin and her stomach drop. Panic and something she hated to admit was a fleeting flash of pity ran through her when she looked at Nina. Iris did her best to push back those emotions, knowing it wasn't what her friend needed at the moment. It was in that instant that Fearnley's earlier words floated to the forefront of her mind.

". . . Let her rest now. She's earned that much."

As Iris looked at Nina, the remnants of her accident still visible in the form of fading cuts and bruises, she couldn't help but agree. Nina's mind had been shattered. The pieces scattered and then hastily put back together only to have the strain of it all threaten to undo it all. The exhaustion and pain—the trauma—was not something Iris could even begin to comprehend.

". . . She's earned that much."

Iris stared at her friend, a bittersweet smile that felt all too fragile spreading across her face, and couldn't help but agree.

"What happened?" Nina asked, on the edge of sleep. Iris just gave a small shake of her head.

"It doesn't matter anymore. Rest," she said, voice soft and tinged with an odd sense of relief—of sadness and hope that all blended into one. It was a tone filled with heartache, much like the smile Iris showed her friend.

Nina took one last look at Iris, closed her eyes, and for the first time in a long while, fell into a peaceful slumber.